Silver Shadows

Silver Shadows

Kate Moseman

Silver Shadows

Copyright © 2021 by Kate Moseman

This is a work of fiction. Names, characters, places, and incidents either are the product of the author's imagination or are used fictitiously. Any resemblance to actual persons, living or dead, events, or locales is entirely coincidental.

First Edition

ISBN 978-1-957320-00-7 (ebook)
ISBN 978-1-957320-01-4 (paperback)

Published by:
Fortunella Press

Nobody is a villain in their own story.

—George R.R. Martin

1

Retirement would either thrill me or kill me; I wasn't sure which when I stepped into the elevator that morning. The red digital numbers ticked higher and higher until the elevator reached my floor: the secretarial hub of Elozent Industries, high above Biscayne Bay and the rest of downtown Miami. Not that our floor was particularly glamorous, but you certainly couldn't beat the view.

The bell dinged, and the elevator doors opened to a roaring sound like a monster grinding palm trees in its teeth. For a moment, I was too startled to move.

The doors slid shut while I hesitated.

I lunged for the button and the doors retreated.

I stepped out.

Thousands of narrow strips of paper littered the floor between overflowing trash bags. A fine and no doubt unhealthy haze of particles hung in the air. And against the wall, where there had been nothing before, a dozen paper shredders ran at full tilt.

My coworkers tottered across the floor with reams of paper and crammed the sheets into the waiting machines. Strands of hair fell from usually neat updos as they scurried about.

One of them staggered past with a stack of paper that threatened to tip. I intercepted her and relieved her of half the stack of paper, then dropped it on a nearby table with a thud. I gestured to the chaos. "What's going on?"

The secretary—another new one, I didn't know her name yet—blew the hair out of her eyes and readjusted her grip on the remaining papers. She shot a look upward, as if it could penetrate to the floors above. "Management. They told us to drop everything and shred."

I pulled a sheet of paper from the pile. Numbers cascaded in meaningless columns. "Why would they—"

She grabbed the paper from my hand and slapped it on the stack. "Don't know. Don't care. If we finish on time, we all get a prize."

"What prize?"

"A fifty dollar gift card each!" She hefted the paper heap and scurried away.

Fifty dollars each? Not bad.

But why the rush?

I made my way over to my desk and sat down. I traded out my New Balance sneakers for work-appropriate heels and picked up the phone.

Time to get to the bottom of this.

I dialed my direct boss. Technically speaking, all of us in the pool could be called on to work for any of the Elozent executives, but I'd been Mauricio's girl Friday—no, a *secretary*; no, an *executive assistant*—long enough for the job title to change several times over. I arranged travel, made copies, scheduled appointments, fielded calls. I got done what the higher-ups didn't feel like doing for themselves. Seniority gave me some immunity to some of the more mindless tasks—like shredding paper—but at the end of the day, I was just another secretary in a pool that was getting younger by the day.

My boss picked up. "Mauricio."

"Mauricio, hey. It's Lenore. What's the deal down here? It looks like a paper factory exploded."

"I know, right?" The sound of papers shuffling carried over the line. "The big bosses are having some kind of fit."

"Do you still want me to make your travel arrangements for the Chicago meeting?"

"Yeah, go ahead. You know how these things go. Everyone freaks out for a couple of days, then it blows over." He sighed. "They gave us free tickets to the company-sponsored Halloween gala at the Hibiscus Museum next week. Now I can't go 'cause I'll be in Chicago."

"Bummer," I said, half-listening as I held the phone between my shoulder and my ear and made a note. "By the way, I'm not shredding paper or cleaning up any of this mess. They can keep the fifty dollar gift card. I'm not contracting a fatal paper cut the week before I retire. And speaking of parties, don't even think about throwing me a party, okay? I don't want a cake, or balloons, or flowers, or a plaque, or—"

"I think you want all those things and you just won't admit it."

"You know what? You can kiss my—"

He laughed. "I think what I'll miss most about you is your sweet, diplomatic nature."

"You know you love me," I said.

"I'll be lost without you."

"Sure you will. You'll miss my sympathetic ear and my incredible ability to make impossible things happen. Now get back to work before I put you on shredding duty, too."

"Yes, ma'am."

I nearly dropped the phone in the cradle, but reversed it at the last second and held it to my ear. "Mauricio?"

"Yes?"

A rolling cart full of paper rattled past. "Keep me posted, okay? In case anything changes."

"You got it."

I hung up and leaned back. I had to admit, I'd miss the excitement just a little. It was one of the reasons I'd stayed at Elozent so long—a big corporation hummed with its own energy, and even though I was just a cog in the machine, I still enjoyed the buzz. And access to the best view in Miami, from an observation deck just off the executive floor.

I should know. I'd snuck up there often enough to have every landmark memorized.

Still, retirement had its charms. I'd sunk my little nest egg into a snug condo downtown, and I'd put some money away in company stock. My Elozent pension, plus Social Security, would cover the rest.

I pulled up my browser. "Chicago . . ." I arranged Mauricio's itinerary on autopilot. Flight, hotel, car. Wash, rinse, repeat.

When the itinerary papers spat out of the nearby printer, I had to leap up and throw myself bodily over the machine before some overeager gift card seeker shredded the printout. I collected the papers and headed for the elevator.

It whisked me skyward and delivered me to the decidedly more upscale executive floor: glass as far as the eye could see, all the way across to the massive windows overlooking downtown Miami and Biscayne Bay. My heels sank a little further into the plush carpet as I crossed the floor.

Mauricio was high enough on the Elozent food chain to merit an office on the executive floor, but not quite high enough to score a window office. He was a good twenty years younger than me, about the same age as my son. I rapped on the office door and opened it without waiting for permission. "Here you go." I laid the papers on his desk.

Mauricio didn't take his eyes off the computer screen. He rubbed his hands over his shaved head. "Thanks," he said.

"Well, I didn't expect a ticker tape parade, but you could actually look up when you speak to me."

Mauricio's lips quirked. He continued to stare at the screen. "Come here for a second, will you?"

I came around the desk and peered at the screen. He had his employee investment account up, similar to the retirement account I'd just been looking at.

"Notice anything?" He clicked around.

"No."

"Exactly."

"So?"

"So, I can't get my account to do anything."

"Must be a glitch."

"Have you been on yours?"

"Last I checked, it was working."

"Did you try to do anything?"

"No, I haven't broken my piggy bank yet, if that's what you're asking. Do you want me to call I.T.?"

He frowned at the screen. "Could you?"

"You got it." I patted his shoulder and moved back to the other side of the desk before turning around. "Want anything else while I'm up here?"

"Cafecito, please. And one for you, if you like."

Executive-level perks, like freshly brewed Cuban coffees, were not to be missed. I stopped by the bar and ordered two.

The uniformed barista prepared them to go and slid them across the polished zinc bar top.

I knocked back my own shot of strong, sweet liquid, dropped off Mauricio's, and returned to the lower floor.

The mood was, if possible, even more shrill than when I'd left. Enough file boxes to build a fort lined the walls. The air reeked of overburdened shredder motors.

"This can't be healthy," I observed, to no one in particular. I tugged my shirt over my nose. I didn't need to acquire some sort of paper-induced lung disease.

Back at my desk, I pulled up my retirement account again. I clicked on *Withdraw Money.*

Nothing happened.

Transfer Money.

Nothing.

Add Money.

The screen obligingly flipped to the next step in the process.

Oh, it would let me do that, would it? But not transfer or withdraw. I picked up the phone and dialed the I.T. department.

A man answered the phone in a bored tone. "Hello, I.T. Have you tried—"

"Do *not* ask me if I've tried turning it off and on again. I'm not in the mood."

Silence on the other end of the line.

"What's going on with the employee investment account site? I can't do anything with it, and neither can my boss."

"I apologize for the inconvenience," he said, in a drone that made it very clear exactly how *un*-apologetic he was. "We are aware of this issue and are working to restore full access as soon as possible."

"Meaning when?"

"I don't have a timeline on that."

"Oh, for—" I propped my head in my hand and silently exhaled the words that had been about to pop out of my mouth. "You don't have a timeline?"

Again, the voice like a robot reading a cue card: "We apologize for the inconvenience and will restore—"

I hung up. "Useless clown."

Retirement was sounding better and better.

2

At the end of the day, I popped on my walking shoes and rode the elevator down to the ground floor. The stale air gave way to a salt-tinged breeze that swirled in off the bay and tossed the fronds of the palm trees lining the sidewalks. Although Miami wasn't as much of a big city as, say, New York, it had its own charms. There were enough tall buildings to give it excitement, but not so many that they blocked the view of the clear blue Florida sky.

I walked home past other towers, trendy nightspots, and chic boutiques with window displays, stopping at one to admire an elegant caped jacket draped stylishly over a faceless mannequin. The camel-colored fabric looked soft enough to snuggle. I wanted to go inside and try it on, but the very young saleswomen had given me funny looks the last time I'd ventured in to look at something that caught my eye. Maybe they thought I was going to steal something.

Or maybe they thought older women couldn't, or shouldn't, wear stylish clothes.

A shift in the clouds changed the lighting, and revealed my reflection in the shop window: no-nonsense white blouse, black skirt, and black blazer.

I touched my hair with my free hand. My roots were showing. I didn't know if I was tired of dyeing it, or if I was just tired of feeling like I *had* to dye it. Worse, the window reflection washed out all the brown color. I looked like a photo negative of myself.

I was too hungry to stand and stare for long, though. I could always come back and try on the jacket later. Better to continue on to the Peruvian takeout place halfway between Elozent and my condo tower.

Why cook when there's takeout?

I placed my order for the usual and received an assortment of boxes loaded into a large brown paper bag. The scent of roast chicken was enough to make me want to pop open the container right then and there, but I was so close to home I managed to restrain myself.

I crossed the street and continued to my building.

It wasn't as ritzy as some of the downtown buildings. The lobby was small and unoccupied, and had that particular scent common to buildings from the 1980s—long-ago air fresheners and gentle decay. A faded Patrick Nagel poster still hung in a gold metal frame on the wall by the elevator. But, I could afford this place on my retirement savings—and that's what really mattered.

I pushed the elevator button, boarded, and rode upwards. A quick walk down the quiet, carpeted hallway, and I was pushing open the door to my condo. I set my bags on the green velvet couch, dodged the table with its mismatched painted chairs—call it shabby chic—and went straight to the window.

Ah, Miami. The Magic City.

Sure, the bay was only a small blue sliver in the corner—downtown buildings blocked the rest—but it was there, and I could see it sparkle if I squinted. The city streets lay below me like my own personal playground. If anything could keep me feeling young, the energy of the city could. Well worth the budget squeeze it took to make my home in the middle of it all.

Six o'clock on the dot, my phone rang.

I sighed. I loved my son, but sometimes he seemed to view himself as my benevolent nanny-slash-dictator. "Hello?"

"Hey, Mom. Did you take your medicine?"

"Not yet, my bouncing baby boy." He was forty.

"I just didn't want you to forget."

I opened the fridge, grabbed a can of Dr. Pepper, and popped the tab. "How could I forget when you call me at the same time every day?"

"I'm not trying to bug you—"

"I'm just yanking your chain, kiddo. How are things?" I took a long pull from my soda.

"Getting ready for the big Trail or Treat event. Trying not to eat all the candy ahead of time."

"Raise a boy in the city, and look what happens. He becomes a park ranger and spends all his time in the woods."

"It's healthy. And you should get out of that skyscraper every once in a while. Some fresh air is good for you."

"I walk to work and back every day, isn't that enough fresh air? Probably fresher than the swamp air you marinate in all day."

"Why don't you drive out this weekend? We can go for a walk on one of the new trails."

"Ugh. You know I hate nature. Too many bugs."

"There's no bugs, Mom—it's October.

"Fine, I'll go walk the un-buggy woods. Now let me go eat, my dinner's getting cold."

"Don't forget your—"

"Medicine, I know. Sheesh."

"Love you."

"You too."

After I hung up, I turned on the TV to keep me company. I removed the stuffed potatoes and the passionfruit cheesecake from the paper tote bag, followed by the rotisserie chicken. I had the rotisserie chicken half out of its box when I heard Elozent Industries mentioned on the evening news. I abandoned the chicken and hurried into the living room in time to catch the Elozent logo blazing across the screen in full color before fading into black-and-white.

"Elozent stock fell at an unprecedented rate today after Elozent CEO Robert Wickham abruptly resigned his position. The U.S. Securities and Exchange Commission has announced an investigation into what analysts predict may become one of the greatest financial scandals of the twenty-first century . . ."

The newscaster said more, but I struggled to understand it over the sudden roar in my ears. I reached for my phone and fumbled for the browser app that would take me to my Elozent retirement account.

A tap, a swipe . . . and I gasped.

The amount had dropped by a third.

I stabbed desperately at the transaction buttons—if I worked fast, maybe I could transfer some funds out—but nothing worked. Instead, a pop-up appeared: "The selected function has been temporarily disabled. We are aware of this issue and are working to restore full access as soon as possible. Please try your transaction again later."

I pulled up my boss's number and mashed the call button. It rang five times before going to voicemail. "Mauricio, it's Lenore. What the hell is going on? Have you seen the news? Have you seen what happened to the stock? Call me back." I hung up and desperately refreshed the account page, trying to get it to do something.

Each time, it remained the same.

I flung down the phone and went to the kitchen, where I shoved the food in the fridge—I'd lost my appetite. Then I pulled a wine glass from the cabinet and poured in a little too much Chardonnay. I carried the full glass back to the living room and watched in numb horror as the news narrated the spectacle of my retirement circling the drain.

They'd told us our investment was a sure thing. That our pensions were guaranteed.

I picked up the phone and tried Mauricio again.

He answered on the second ring. "Lenore, I can't talk now."

"No—don't hang up—a third of my retirement is gone!"

"Can you get the rest out?"

"No, it's still—"

"Frozen," he finished, sounding grim. "I know. I tried too."

I swallowed a large gulp of wine. "Maybe it's just a temporary dip."

Silence on the other end of the line.

"Mauricio?"

"I have to go."

"No, don't fob me off with that! You're higher up than I am—you *know* things. Tell me the truth!"

"I'm in the same boat as you." He paused. "Get your money out if you can."

The line went dead.

I screeched with frustration, then refreshed the retirement account. In the time it had taken to get no answers from Mauricio, the total amount had gone down to less than half of what it had been that morning.

The room spun gently and appeared to pitch slightly sideways. The Chardonnay I'd just swallowed threatened to reappear. I carefully put down my wineglass on the coffee table. If I was going to die, I refused to ruin the furniture in the process.

I leaned back on the couch and gave in to the insistent spinning sensation. Had I come all this way—left my hometown, cut ties with my family—only to end up a failure at the end of it all?

I was the one who was going to make it big in the city. I was the one who was better than our tiny, boring, sleepy town. Wouldn't they all just laugh to know what was happening to old Lenore.

I squeezed my eyes shut, but that didn't stop the laughter that rang in my head.

I grunted as I stood up. It took two hands on the walls to stay upright as I made my way down the hallway to the tiny linen closet.

The folding door slid back.

Instead of towels, there were books. Dozens of them, old and new. Books I'd collected quietly over the decades, along with an assortment of neatly packed boxes.

But not just any books.

Spellbooks.

Mostly from used bookstores—except for *So You Have Magical Powers*, the one I'd stolen from my witch of a sister before I left town.

Her smug voice echoed in my mind: *That's not how it works, Lenore. You don't have the magic. You'll never have the magic.*

"Shut up," I said. I hauled as many as I could carry to the living room, then returned for the rest. Surely one of them would make a difference—restore my bank account, or my job, or Elozent itself; I didn't care as long as I came out the other side solvent.

With everything in haphazard piles around the living room, I picked up a book and scanned the index. "G for good fortune? M for money?" I ran my finger down the pages until I found a match. "Bingo." I opened to the relevant page and laid it on the table, then grabbed the next book. "L for luck?" The pages riffled under my fingers. "Gotcha." The book joined the first on the coffee table. I kept going until I couldn't even see the coffee table under the array of books. I ringed the rest of the books around the coffee table base until I ran out of space to move around. The remainder went on the couch.

When the last of the volumes lay open before me, I stood back and admired my handiwork. The room gave one more gentle rotation as the Chardonnay buzz settled into a light hum.

The voice, again: *Magic isn't something you can print on a page. You either have it, or you don't.*

"I said shut up! No one asked you!" I shoved the past firmly out my mind and examined the spells one by one. Many called for common kitchen items, like herbs, spices, or oils. Others required money or perfume. Candles, too. I snagged the boxes I'd brought out from the closet and pawed through the contents.

There were candles by the handful, along with crystals and carvings and other bric-a-brac I'd picked up at weird little shops, dusty flea markets, and the occasional online purchase.

My collection.

After making a master list of all the ingredients I needed for the spells, I realized I was missing one unusual item.

One of the spells in *So You Have Magical Powers* called for a key. Not just any key, though. According to the book, it had to be a key that was already enchanted.

The spell would "unlock power," whatever that meant. Sounded pretty good to me, though. I could use some power.

I cleared a spot on the couch and sat. Where would I find an already enchanted key? I certainly couldn't get it in time to cast all the spells that night, which was my plan.

Surely I could let that one spell go. In fact, I kept telling myself that while I lined up the ingredients and items I did have in my possession. But letting go felt painfully close to giving up, so I opened an auction app on my phone and typed "magical key" in the search box.

The listings numbered in the thousands: children's toys, magic shop novelties, and more Santa door keys than you could shake a stick at. Not helpful. But how to narrow it down?

I eliminated anything new—no real magical key worth its salt would be brand new—and anything outside the country. I didn't want to wait on international shipping.

After pages of scrolling, I'd still found nothing but cheap keychains and assorted junk. I considered abandoning that particular spell; after all, I had dozens more to cast. But something—it might have been the Chardonnay—told me to keep going.

On the last page of the search results, some thousand items deep, I found it. The listing was titled *Magical Key–Caution! Serious Practitioners Only*. The subtitle underneath contained only one word: *CURSED*.

I snickered. Cursed, sure. Whatever.

Price: $9.99. A bargain.

The single blurry photo triggered a strange sense of déjà vu—but I'd never seen the silvery key before in my life.

I scanned the item description. "Considered a cursed item . . . blah, blah, blah . . . unpredictable results . . . yada, yada, yada. Sounds potent." I checked the location. "It's in Florida? Done. Take my money." I tapped *Buy It Now*. I put the phone aside and returned my attention to the spellbooks surrounding me. "Now, who wants to go first?"

3

The alarm clock jolted me out of strange dreams the next morning. I staggered down the hall, regretting every ounce of wine I'd had the night before—and then, to add injury to insult, I stubbed my toe on a stack of books I'd left on the living room floor.

I limped into the kitchen and wished, for the first time, that I kept a coffee maker in the house rather than rely on the little sidewalk cafes for my caffeine fix. I drew a glass of tap water instead and knocked it back.

The mess of books and spell components beckoned me to clean it up, but I was too anxious to do something as dull as cleaning.

I needed answers. I needed proof that somewhere within me lay the spark of power. Sure, I'd never cast a spell before in my life, but with the number of spells I'd attempted, something *had* to work.

It had to.

I opened the retirement account app and held my breath while it loaded.

The balance numbers spun like a slot machine and slid into place one by one.

Zero.

Zero.

Zero.

I cried out and dropped the phone. Good thing the kitchen countertop was in reach, because I folded over it like I'd been punched.

"Damn it!" Of course none of the so-called "spells" had worked. What an idiot I'd been to believe they would. Foolish hopefulness, accumulating all those books and crystals and *garbage* like they were some kind of secret treasure.

Just because the magic worked for *her*—no, why torture myself? Why even think about it?

I fumbled under the cabinet for a trash bag and shook it open with a boom like a crack of thunder. "Make a fool of me, will you?" I stuffed the books into the bag, not caring that their covers twisted or bent on the way in. The crystals, candles, figurines, and trinkets followed. "There is no. Such. Thing. As. Magic!" I hurled the full bag away. It slammed against the door.

My breath came heavy into the morning silence. "Not for me, anyway," I added quietly.

I showered and dressed. The brilliant blue autumn sky mocked me on the walk to the Elozent tower—by any rights, the sky should have been filled with lightning and thunder.

In the Elozent plaza, the company's stylized "E" sculpture glinted in the rising sun. People milled around holding cardboard boxes, looking lost. I recognized the barista from the executive floor.

Those who didn't have boxes rushed the glass doors.

I joined the throng and pushed into an elevator. The tang of sweat and fear soured the air. Every time the doors opened, they opened on pandemonium. My stomach jolted with every stop.

At the thirtieth floor, I stepped free of the airless box.

Unshredded papers covered the floor like oversized fallen leaves. Abandoned bags of paper shreds tilted on their sides, spilling their guts across the carpeted floor. Some employees wept openly as they collected their belongings into empty file boxes. Others grabbed everything that wasn't nailed down—from rolling chairs to fax machines.

When I reached my desk, the only thing left of the phone was the wires. I didn't bother to swap my sneakers for heels. I needed to talk to Mauricio, and I couldn't stomach the thought of taking the elevator again, so I headed for the stairs. My steps echoed in the empty stairwell. "Oh, to be young again," I puffed, but I made it to the executive floor.

Unlike my floor, the executive offices were eerily quiet. "Mauricio?" I called.

I walked through the empty halls until I reached his office. The door was ajar. "Mauricio?" I pushed open the door.

Mauricio sat at his desk with his head in his hands. The white sleeves of his dress shirt were messily rolled up, and his tie hung askew. A half-empty bottle of whisky sat on his desk next to an elegant cut crystal tumbler.

I picked up the tumbler and moved it out of reach. "I think it's a little early to start on this, don't you?"

He didn't say anything. When he lifted his head, his eyes were bloodshot. He reached for the bottle, put it to his lips, and took a slug.

I grabbed at the whisky. The contents splashed on the desk, but I managed to pull the bottle out of his hands. "You're not even a drinker. Come on. Let's get some coffee."

"Gone," he mumbled.

"Upsa-daisy." I hauled him out of the chair and propelled him out of the office.

We made it to the abandoned coffee bar with its shining steel espresso machine. I maneuvered Mauricio to a stool and made my way behind the bar. I pushed the on button and gave my red-eyed boss a once-over while I waited for the machine to warm up. He looked like he'd slept in his clothes.

When the lights illuminated on the machine, I copied the steps I'd seen the barista do a thousand times: fill the portafilter basket, tamp the grounds, twist the portafilter into the head, line up a cup, push the button.

The machine burbled and hissed. A stream of brown liquid trickled into the cup, and the brewing ceased with a lifelike sigh.

"Voilà. Espresso à la Lenore." I pushed the cup into Mauricio's hands.

He drank it without changing expression.

I made one for myself and leaned on the bar. "Now tell me what the hell's going on. You never called me back last night. How bad is it?"

"Worse than you can imagine."

"You'd be surprised what I can imagine."

Mauricio took a deep breath and set his cup on the bar. "They were falsifying the income reports. Making it look like we were doing better than ever."

"For how long?"

"Years."

I whistled.

"The stock kept going up and up," he said, "until it didn't. The execs at the top knew it was coming. They cashed out at the last second—emptied the pension fund, too—and left the rest of us to twist in the wind."

"And all that money . . ."

"Gone."

I felt like I'd been punched. "Elozent Industries was supposed to be rock solid. Everyone said it was—even the Wall Street Journal, for God's sake!"

"Everyone was wrong."

We both fell silent.

I remembered the family photos on his desk. "What are you going to do?"

"Do?" He shrugged. "I can't *do* anything but start over." He looked at me and his brow knitted. "What about you?"

"Me?" A brittle laugh escaped my lips. "Oh, I'm sure it's easy to start over in your sixties after your retirement fund has been nuked."

"Have you told your son?"

"Hell, no." He didn't need to worry about me any more than he already did.

"What about the rest of your family?"

"I'd rather live in a cardboard box than ask my sister for help."

An unfamiliar voice pierced the empty floor. "May I have your attention, please. Elozent Industries is subject to seizure. This property will be locked in thirty minutes. Please exit at this time. Thank you."

I glanced at the ceiling. "I didn't even know we had an announcement system."

Mauricio shook his head. "They made that announcement earlier, right before you came in. Only there was more time left, then."

"No wonder everyone was grabbing everything that wasn't nailed down." I surveyed the bar. "Need any dishware?"

He let out a pained laugh.

I rapped my knuckles on the counter. "Go get your things before we all get thrown out."

"Yes, ma'am." He stretched and stood up.

"And, hey—"

Mauricio faced me.

"Knock off the sauce. Your family needs you." I set the empty coffee cup in the sink and walked away.

"I didn't know you cared," he called.

I flipped him the bird over my shoulder.

His voice reached me once more as I pushed open the stairwell door. "Take care of yourself, Lenore," he called.

"Oh, I'll take care, all right," I muttered. "I'll take care of whoever's responsible for this."

4

The next morning, I didn't bother to put on an outfit when I got out of bed. What was the point of changing out of my pajamas just to haul my trash out to the condo's dumpster? Who cared if the neighbors thought I was an eccentric old lady?

I rummaged through the sad cardboard file box of remnants from my job. The box held a stapler that tended to jam, an unopened set of Elozent sticky notes, a mug full of Elozent pens, and—in an apparent attempt to murder irony—an Elozent-branded stress ball.

Oh, great. I'd forgotten my favorite pair of heels under my desk.

I saved the notes and the pens and stamped the box flat to fit in the previous day's trash bag. I rode the elevator down to the ground floor and crossed the parking lot, blinking in unfiltered light of a cloudless sky.

I held up the lid of the dumpster and pushed the bag inside. The lid slammed shut with the finality of a coffin. When I turned to go inside, an assortment of urchins blocked my path.

Right. It was Saturday—kids were out of school.

Just what I needed first thing in the morning.

"Hey, lady," said the closest one, a boy with a mop of hair and a shiny silver scooter. "Is that your Halloween costume?" he said, with what seemed like genuine curiosity.

I glanced down at the pink cotton button-down top and matching pajama pants, both emblazoned with palm trees and colorful cocktails. "Yeah, what of it?"

"I'm going to be Thanos."

"Who?"

"You know, from the Avengers movie?" The boy cocked his head. "He gets rid of half the people by snapping his fingers?"

"Oh, *that* Thanos. Sounds like a great role model. Good luck with that." I slipped past and headed for the building entrance.

Kids.

I spent the rest of the morning in fruitless pursuit of justice—or really, when it came down to it, money. I called lawyers, banks, legal aid societies, senior citizen groups, and local newspapers, to no avail. I was nobody special, just one of the thousands of Elozent employees left in the lurch.

And of course all of Elozent's creditors would want a piece of the pie, too—except the pie had been dropped off the top of the Elozent building. We'd all be crawling around on our hands and knees trying to scrape up the remnants.

Until something like a class action lawsuit was launched, I'd just have to cool my heels. I considered opening another bottle of Chardonnay, but decided it would be a bad idea to go the Mauricio route. No more Chardonnay for me.

A rustling sound at the door interrupted my thoughts.

I opened the door to find a small padded envelope on the doorstep. I scooped it up and closed the door, wondering what it could be. It was too tough to tear open, so I retrieved a pair of scissors, cut off one end of the envelope, and upended it.

An old-fashioned silver key fell into my hand.

I groaned. The key. A reminder of the other night's colossal failure. I stuffed the envelope into the trash and held the trash can lid open to let the key follow the envelope.

But just as I was about to release it, a piercing pain zipped through my fingers, as fast and intense as a wasp sting.

I yelled and threw the key across the room. It clattered against the far wall and fell to the floor.

I peered at my hand. The pads of my thumb and index fingers, where I'd held the key, had turned a rosy red shade.

I crossed the room and found the key where it had fallen to the floor under the window. This time, I folded the cuff of my pink pajama sleeve over it before I picked it up by the ornate silver handle. The bit wouldn't have fit any modern lock. "Maybe you're not trash, after all." I gave it an experimental prod with one finger.

Nothing happened.

I wasn't sure if that was an improvement on the stinging sensation or not.

I ran a fingertip down the shank.

It *vibrated*.

I set down the key on the table, hurried to the trash can, and tugged out the packaging. The envelope was completely empty. No receipt, no user's manual, nothing. I flipped over the envelope to look at the front. No return address, either.

Come to think of it—why had it been delivered to my door? It should have easily fit in my mailbox downstairs.

Or, it would have—

If there had been any postage on it.

I opened the auction app on my phone. I pulled up the transaction and clicked on the seller link—but it only took me to an error page. Whoever had sold the key had vanished.

Maybe the key wasn't really magic. Maybe the sting and the vibration were all in my head.

That's not how it works, Lenore.

Or maybe the universe had given me one more shot.

I rushed downstairs. Behind the building, the tiny maintenance shed yielded a ladder, which I hauled over to the dumpster.

The kids doing scooter tricks stopped to watch. "Whatcha doin', lady?" called the boy, also known as Thanos.

"Come hold this steady," I replied.

He scootered over, skidded to a stop, and dropped the scooter to the ground.

I propped the ladder against the dumpster and stepped onto the first rung.

The boy grasped the ladder from the side.

I was climbing into a dumpster. It was madness.

I kept going anyway.

At the top edge of the dumpster, I eased one leg over. The bag I'd discarded was almost in reach. "This would be a really stupid way to die," I observed.

I hooked my foot around the top of the bag and knocked it closer. The half-open bag was in reach, and although there was no way I could haul the whole thing down the ladder, I could at least retrieve the book I wanted. I shook the bag open and threw aside one book after another until I had the one with the spell that called for a magical key. "*So You Have Magical Powers*. Bingo." I tossed the book to the boy. Then I carefully climbed down the ladder. "Thank you," I said when my slippers touched the ground.

He eyed the book. "No problem." He turned the book over, as if to read the back.

I tugged it out of his grasp. "Don't you have someplace to be?"

He shrugged. "I was just waiting to see what you would do next."

"I'm going to go cast a magic spell."

His face scrunched as he considered this revelation. "For Halloween?"

"Sure, why not." I tucked the book under my arm and lowered the ladder to a carrying position. "See you around, Thanos." Once I'd stashed the ladder back in the maintenance shed, I returned to my condo—and washed myself thoroughly. I didn't need to contract dumpster mange on top of everything else.

Freshly scrubbed and fully dressed, I opened the rescued book. On closer inspection, it was more like a thick booklet you might make at a local copy shop. Not a lot of pages.

I ran my finger down the component list. In addition to a magical key—check—I needed a candle, a cauldron, a piece of paper, and an ink pen. "Blue or black?" I mused aloud. "Eh, I'm sure it's fine either way." I grabbed one of the Elozent pens.

Problem was, I'd chucked all my special witchy candles in the trash. And a *cauldron*? How had I missed *that* on the first read? Must have been the Chardonnay.

"Cauldron, cauldron . . ." I tapped my chin with the pen. "Aha!" I stood up and went to the kitchen. I hung on to the countertop and lowered myself to kneel next to the oven. A sharp tug, and the oven drawer slid open to reveal a cast iron pan, someone's idea of a housewarming gift that had never seen the light of day. I set the heavy pan on the counter and stood up.

The only candle left was the one I kept in the bathroom, a souvenir from a long ago vacation to Sanibel Island. It still had the lid on; I'd never even lit the wick. I picked it up and whipped off the lid. "Candle!"

With the pan, the candle, the pen, and the key on the dining table, I was almost ready. "Paper." I looked around the room.

The fluorescent Post-It notes practically shouted, "Use me!"

I unwrapped a pack and added it to the dining table. The spellbook text was small, and printed in some kind of compressed italics, so I had to stop and find my reading glasses. Then I read the spell instructions aloud: "'Touch the key to the earth.'" I looked around. "Does a potted plant count?"

I grabbed a wilted pothos plant and stuck the key into the dirt like sticking a key into a car ignition. I pulled it out. "Earth—done. Now what? 'Rinse the key in water.' Well, naturally, now that I've made a mess of it."

I carried the key to the kitchen and rinsed it in the sink.

The aroma of earth faded. In its place, the light scent of rain arose from the sink.

"Water—done. What's next?" I returned to the book. "'Write the word 'unlock' on the paper. Wrap the key in the paper and place it in the cauldron.'" I scribbled the word on the Post-It and wrapped the Post-It around the key—the sticky strip came in handy for that—and put the wrapped key in the cast iron pan. "Done." I scanned the rest of the directions: "Light the paper and let it burn to ash."

I had to stop again and get some matches.

Facing the cast iron pan, I lit the match and touched it to the paper.

The Post-It curled into ash and scraps. I lit another match and burned the scraps, just to be sure. "Fire—done." I expected to feel something—a rush of energy, perhaps, or a tingling sense of newfound power coursing through my veins—but all I really felt was an overwhelming urge to take a nap. I scooped up the key, which was still warm, and blew off the ashes. With the key in my hand, the pressure to sleep turned unstoppable.

I collapsed to the couch with the silver key firmly in my grasp.

5

My mouth tasted like metal, and the light from the window was the cold gray color of the pre-dawn sky. I'd slept away the afternoon and most of the night. My fingers hurt. I looked down to find them still curled around the key. I loosened my aching joints and dropped the key on the coffee table with a clatter that sounded loud in the stillness of the early morning.

Another day, another lack of dollars.

I stretched, stood, and plucked the key from the table. "What power have you unlocked, huh? Air, fire, water, or earth?" I held it out like a tiny wand and concentrated. "Come on, wind power. Give me a breeze. A little draft. Just a puff."

The key didn't zap me, but then again, it didn't do anything at all.

"Damn." I held it out again. "Let's try fire." I pivoted to the cast iron pan, balled up a piece of paper, and dropped it in. "Flame on!"

Nothing.

I shook the key like a mercury thermometer and pointed it right at the paper. "Burn?"

It did not burn.

I moved to the kitchen sink and turned on the water. "Water powers, activate!"

The tap ran and ran with no sign of magical interference.

"I command you to splash?"

Nothing.

"They really should write a manual for these things." I grabbed the yellowing pothos and pointed the key at its ailing leaves. "Earth magic, go, go . . ."—I was starting to run out of intelligent thoughts—"grow!"

The pothos plant did not, in fact, grow. Or go. Or do anything that would indicate it had been affected in the tiniest bit.

I held the key up to my face. "So what are you good for, then, if you can't summon the elements?" I shook the key like I could shake some sense into it. "Maybe I should melt you down, huh? Is that what you want?"

ZAP.

"Ow!" I wrung my hand. I peered at the key in the strengthening sunlight. It didn't look any different, and it didn't seem to do very much, but the desire to keep it close gripped me. I headed down the hallway, dug around in my dresser, and found an old leather cord. The key slid on easily, and after I knotted the cord, I hung the makeshift pendant around my neck and under my shirt. The metal was alternately warm and cool on my skin, like it couldn't make up its mind. "I'll figure you out yet. And then we'll see what we can do."

My phone buzzed once.

My son had sent a text: *You up?*

Yes, why? I wrote.

You busy?

I rolled my eyes and hit the dial button to continue the conversation by phone. "Why do you ask?" I said, when he picked up.

"I thought you might like to go for that walk with me this morning."

"In the woods? On a Sunday?"

"No, in the mall on a Tuesday," he replied, deadpan. "Of course in the woods."

"You're not going to leave me alone until I go, are you?"

"Nope."

Maybe I did need some fresh air to clear my mind. Fresh air could be healthier than maintaining a depressive relationship with the couch and the TV. "Ugh, fine. But only because you twisted my arm. And if there are any bugs out there, I'm holding you personally responsible."

"I'll see you at Black Mangrove Preserve." He hung up.

I couldn't be mad; he really was the nicest kind of bully. I put on my sneakers like an obedient child and went down to my little silver two-door sedan.

I navigated through the canyons of downtown Miami, past the palm trees that punctuated the sidewalks, under the Metrorail line and Interstate 95, through Little Havana, and into the sprawl of the outlying suburbs.

The change from city to swamp happened quickly. One minute, everything was covered in concrete; the next, greens and browns as far as the eye could see. The canal running alongside the road looked like it had been brewing a cruise ship-sized tea bag for a thousand years.

I passed sign after sign advertising Everglades airboat tours. I kept going until I reached the turnoff for Black Mangrove Preserve.

The parking lot was uncrowded, most likely because it was the off-season between the summer tourists and the holiday snowbirds. The glass-encased information board held a sun-faded map, a list of park rules, and a jointed Halloween witch decoration that had seen better days. I snagged a brochure and looked around for my son.

He was leaning on the railing of the promenade by the river. He may not have been on duty, but he still favored tough-looking khakis.

"Sheridan!"

He turned, revealing his t-shirt of the day: multicolored tree silhouettes on a black background—with an astronaut floating above, holding a dripping ice cream cone and a boombox.

Typical Sheridan-wear. And no matter how much he tried to calm his hair, it still tumbled in all directions.

I waved vigorously.

He waved back and crossed the clearing between the promenade and the parking lot.

As was so often the case, we were meeting from completely opposite directions. I hugged him. "Nice shirt."

"You like it?" He peered down at his shirt like it was the first time he'd seen it, then gestured ahead. "The new trail is this way."

We veered out of the clearing and entered an elevated wooden walkway that smelled of fresh-cut lumber. Towering trees draped with Spanish moss closed in on all sides.

"So, are you excited about retiring next week?" he asked.

I blinked. He either hadn't seen the news, or he didn't think it affected me. Good. "Oh, yeah," I said, forcing an easy-sounding cheer. "That's the brass ring, isn't it? Retirement?"

His brow furrowed. "I know we talked about how you might be—well—bored."

I smiled to myself. Sheridan could be such a blunt creature. "Of course not, kiddo. I'll be living la vida loca." A lie was far better than dropping the truth on him. He'd think he had to take care of me—or move me in. Perish the thought.

"You said you might travel."

That I had. I'd made big plans, all of which were now in the dumpster like my Elozent stress ball.

Sheridan stopped to observe something making noise in the grass below the walkway.

I kept strolling while I tried to come up with a better response than what I was thinking: *I'd like to travel right out of this stupid world and into someplace where money doesn't matter.*

The key on my chest pulsed.

The air cooled and stilled like I had stepped into a movie theater. The yellowish wood color of the boardwalk faded before my eyes to the bleached shade of driftwood. The color leached from the trees, turning brown trunks and green leaves to silvery shades of black and white. Every single sound disappeared: no wind in the branches, no splashes in the nearby water, no bird calls. No distant traffic noise.

A shiver crept over my skin. I turned toward Sheridan, who had been a few steps behind me. "What is going on—"

He was gone.

I grabbed the railing. "Sheridan?" I whipped around, looking back along the trail.

No one.

My heart raced. I placed a hand on my chest and tried to breathe slowly. "It's okay, I'm just having some kind of . . . episode. It'll be fine." A glance in the opposite direction of the trail revealed nothing but more silvery wetland. "Maybe I've passed out. That's it—I've passed out, and I'll wake up any second now, and Sheridan will be right there, fanning me with a park brochure."

I leaned over the railing, as if Sheridan might have leaped to the swamp below.

Obviously not.

I clung to the railing and wobbled my way back to the trail entrance one shaky step at a time. The oppressive silence made my heartbeat loud in my ears.

Everything was black and white, like an old movie, but horribly still. Even the smell of swamp water had disappeared. There was no one in sight. I longed for a sign of life—a bird, a squirrel, even a mosquito—anything at all to interrupt the metallic silence.

What if I wasn't unconscious?

What if this was real?

What if I was dying?

My stomach pitched. I ran to the promenade beside the water and leaned over the railing in time to empty my stomach into the mirrorlike water.

I spat to clear my mouth. "Pull yourself together, Lenore. You're not dying." I almost believed it, so I kept talking to myself. "You've handled worse. You left your home. You were a single mom. You lost your entire retirement and you didn't have a breakdown—well, not much of one, anyway." I pulled the key from beneath my shirt and held it in my hand. "You wanted magic, didn't you?"

Magic isn't something you can print on a page. You either have it, or you don't.

The magic I remembered . . . it was nothing like this.

But could this be something new?

The key didn't zap or buzz, but it seemed to shimmy as if it were somehow pleased with itself.

"This is your fault, isn't it? You've done something to me. And Sheridan. And"—I gestured at my surroundings—"Florida." The high-contrast wetland landscape looked like nothing so much as an Ansel Adams print carved out of shadows and light.

I wasn't unconscious, or having a stroke. My son wasn't gone—he just wasn't *here.*

This was some kind of *travel.*

Just not the kind I'd had in mind.

I held the key tighter. "Listen, key—I want to go back to the real world."

No sooner had the words left my lips than the whole world flipped. Monochromatic objects blazed with color again. A breeze brushed my hair, and a blue heron continued its slow-motion stalking in the grass. I stood in exactly the same spot where I'd stopped on the promenade beside the open river.

There was no evidence I'd been sick.

My head spun. I leaned on the railing and rested my head on my arms.

Footsteps thumped on the promenade. "Mom!" Sheridan's breathless cry came from behind me. "Where did you go? I thought you fell over the side or something!"

I lifted my head and tried to look normal. "No, no, I'm fine. I—uh—needed to use the bathroom."

His eyebrows shot up. "How'd you get past me? And the restrooms are over by the ranger station."

I considered saying, *Well, you see, I was sucked into some kind of dead black-and-white world*, but he was probably already halfway to thinking I needed to be put in a home and I didn't need that to go any further. I drew myself up with perfect dignity. "You didn't see me walk past because you were looking away from me. And then, on the way to the ladies' room, I stopped to take a picture of this blue heron." I pulled out my phone and carefully snapped a picture of the bird.

His gaze shifted from me, to the bird, and back again. "Right." His confused expression cleared slowly, leaving behind a trace of disbelief. "Did you want to go to the bathroom before we go back on the trail?"

I didn't want to go to the bathroom. Now that I was out of wherever-it-was, my fear slid sideways into a strange kind of excitement. My mind raced. All I could think was: *My will is up-to-date.*

Might as well experiment.

6

I'm sure I was terrible company, distracted as I was, but I did my best to keep up a steady stream of chatter to reassure Sheridan while we completed our trail walk. He gave me another funny look before we parted, but he let me go after I promised to meet up again soon.

It was sweet, really, how he worried about me. All the more reason not to tell him what was really going on. What would I even say? "Hi, kiddo. Your Mom's going off to explore the dangerous unknown. Yes, I'll remember to take my medication. Bye!"

He'd think I lost my marbles.

No. If I did this, I'd have to do it alone.

I sped back downtown on the Tamiami Trail.

In the parking lot, under the lengthening shadow beneath my condominium tower, I turned off the ignition and pulled the mysterious key out from under my shirt. There was something strange about all of this. After so many decades of wanting real magic—to have it dropped in my lap like this—it was as daunting as it was exciting.

Did I dare go back to the black-and-white world? I'd gotten in and out easily enough, but maybe there were other dangers. Colorless terrors lurking in the shadows.

But really—was it a choice at all? How could I close the door on the greatest mystery, the greatest adventure I'd ever been presented with?

The truth was, I'd have had to throw the key in a lake to stop myself.

I took a deep breath. There was no one in sight. No one to see me disappear into wherever-it-was. To be on the safe side, I hunkered down across the front seats, out of view, and clutched the key. "I want to go back to the shadow world."

At first, it seemed like nothing happened. The black interior of my sedan didn't look noticeably different. I slowly turned my head up to look out the windshield.

The blue October sky had washed into a moon-colored grayish white. The palm trees had turned gray like an old Miami picture postcard. An odd light seemed to come from nowhere and everywhere.

I sat up. Out of curiosity, I turned the car key in the ignition.

The engine didn't turn over; in fact, the ignition didn't even make that clicking sound it makes when the battery is dead.

I removed the car key and stowed my normal, un-magical keys in my purse.

Now what?

I opened the door slowly and got out of the car. After a moment's hesitation, I put my purse over my shoulder. Maybe it was silly to carry it into a world seemingly devoid of people—if I left it in my car, who would steal it?—but it felt stranger to abandon it. The car door slammed shut with a muted thump.

Tall buildings surrounded the parking lot, just as they always did, but their windows reflected that steady, cool, omnipresent light, rather than the natural, tumbling colors of clouds and sunlight.

I crossed the lot to the sidewalk bordering what would normally have been a busy roadway. Instead of stop-and-go traffic, the cars sat in the road as if they'd been abandoned.

I tried the door of a Camaro. It opened easily. I slid into the bucket seat, ran my hands over the leather steering wheel, and felt around for the keys. They hung from the ignition, but swiveling them back and forth got me no more results than when I'd tried starting my own car.

I got out and tried another car door, then another. All the doors were unlocked, but none of the engines worked.

Weird.

I left the street and entered the nearest shop: Parallel 26, the one with the caped jacket in the window.

The lights didn't seem to be on. Instead, the same diffused glow that lit the sky also permeated the shop interior. Although the light had seemed eerie at first, the longer I was exposed to it, the more it resembled the soothing glow of an overcast sky.

I crossed the sales floor and entered the narrow hallway of fitting rooms, two on the left and two on the right. One thing I knew about Parallel 26 was that you had to get an associate to unlock a fitting room. I pushed down on the handle of the first fitting room door.

Click. The door swung silently open, showing my full-length black-and-white reflection in the mirror.

The next door, *click*.

The third door, *click*.

By the time I pushed the fourth door open, I was laughing. "Guess I don't need to ask someone to unlock it!"

I returned to the racks of clothing. The swing coat, the same as the one in the window, hung temptingly from a polished wood hanger.

As if in a dream, I slipped the coat off the hanger and over my shoulders. It melted around me like butter and caressed me like stolen kisses. "Oh," I murmured. "That's very nice."

Could I take it? Would it disappear when I re-entered the real world?

I stroked the soft collar.

Did I have it in me to walk out of a store with a coat I didn't own?

The silent air hung around me, cool and neutral, without judgment.

First, I should try something small.

I took off the coat and replaced it on the hanger.

At the checkout counter, I found a display of fine chocolate: bars, truffles, and seasonal shapes. I picked up a foil-wrapped chocolate pumpkin and held it to my nose.

Strangely, it had no scent.

I unwrapped the stem to reveal the gray chocolate underneath. Still no chocolate aroma. I couldn't bring myself to taste it. Instead, I pressed the foil shut and slipped the chocolate pumpkin into my purse.

A little rush swept through me, like I'd crossed an illicit threshold.

I kind of liked it.

I anchored my purse securely over my shoulder and walked out. I looked up and down the street before crossing the road, out of habit, but with all of the cars in silent stasis, I could have danced the merengue down the center line if I wanted to.

I entered the condo lobby through the unlocked door and punched the elevator button out of habit. But the hum of the elevator's descent did not come, nor did the shiny metallic doors open.

I peered at the elevator button. Had it even lit up? I smacked it a few times for good measure.

Did elevators not work in the shadow world?

The woman in the Patrick Nagel poster glared at me with sharply-drawn eyes.

The truth hit me when I recalled how the car wouldn't turn over. It wasn't that elevators didn't work—*electricity* didn't work. No elevators, no cars. And no lights or air conditioning, either, but I hadn't noticed because of the weird ambient light and the stable, slightly chilled temperature.

That presented a puzzle.

To reappear in the real world meant that I would reappear out of nothing, possibly within sight of others, who I couldn't see before I switched over. No matter where I went, who knew what would be there when I reappeared?

The only way to return safely would be to do so in an environment where I could be sure no one could come in or out.

For that reason, it seemed smart to go back to my condo, where I knew I would be alone when I switched over from this strange world to the real one.

But how could I get to my condo in the shadow world without an elevator to carry me? The idea of climbing fifteen flights didn't appeal.

If I went back to the Parallel 26 fitting room to make the transition, I couldn't just pop out of a previously unoccupied room. I didn't want to draw attention to myself, especially not after I'd stolen a chocolate pumpkin.

That left my little old sedan. Sure, it wasn't the most elegant solution, but if I hunkered down in the front seat—out of sight—chances were good that no one would notice anything out of the ordinary.

I returned to my car. It was awkward to hunch over the front seat, but better than staying upright and popping back into full view. The key dangled from its leather cord and rested on the passenger seat fabric.

"I want to go back."

Nothing happened.

My heart skipped a beat. Why didn't it work? I sat up and the key fell against my chest.

Oh. I didn't seem to need to hold the key to make it work, but maybe it did need to be touching my skin. I shoved the key down my shirt and held it in place as I bent down again. "I want to go back," I said firmly.

The quality of the light immediately changed. Instead of a sunless white sky, the car interior baked in the light of the autumn sun.

I sat up cautiously. Everything appeared to be just as it had been before. My stomach rumbled loudly—I hadn't eaten anything since before going out with Sheridan—so I rummaged in my purse for the chocolate pumpkin.

It wasn't there.

I plunged my fingers into every nook, cranny, and zippered pocket.

No chocolate pumpkin.

I struck the steering wheel. I could bring myself in and out of the gray world, but it looked like I wouldn't be able to bring any souvenirs. Either way, I wouldn't be doing any more experimenting until I got something to eat, so I got out of the car and headed for the lobby.

Thanos Boy zipped in front of me on his silver scooter. "Where did you come from?"

I froze. Surely he hadn't seen. "What do you mean?"

His face scrunched up. "You weren't in your car."

I laughed. "Of course I was. You just didn't see me, that's all."

He leaned on the handlebars, seemingly unfazed. "Are you some kind of a witch, for real?"

I turned my face to the sky, letting the real sun warm my skin, and gave my best imitation of a harmless old woman indulging a child's whimsy.

"Maybe I am."

7

The evening news made a field day out of the Elozent collapse. Each channel had its own spin on how the executives had slowly hollowed out the company from the inside, but all of the channels had pictures and video of Robert Wickham, the CEO, who had kept smiling for the cameras right up until the end.

And after that, he'd flown to his Andros Island estate, in the Bahamas, leaving his Miami mansion unoccupied.

There'd been some kind of magazine feature about his house a few years back; I remembered because it was water cooler talk for a day or two at work. I searched for the article on my phone and found it: "Modern Luxe on Biscayne Bay: A Stunning Retreat."

The house looked like a very expensive stack of concrete shoeboxes nestled in lush green landscaping. Gigantic windows stretched two stories high. Inside, modern furniture in rich leather and polished wood punctuated the spacious living area. Contemporary paintings vied for attention with vintage statuary. Exotic stone was *everywhere*—the walls, the floors, the countertops.

So much money you could practically smell it from the photos.

From my perch on the worn velvet couch, I spared a glance at my mismatched dining chairs, and kept reading.

The Wickhams—he was married—collected art to fill their lavish home. I had to wonder what kind of jewelry the wife must have had. And what it was worth.

It wasn't hard to find the exact house on a map. I zoomed in. The Wickham house was located on Sun Island, one of the sand-dredged man-made islands in Biscayne Bay, barely a stone's throw from downtown. A little too far to walk, but if I wanted to get there, I could park in a commercial area nearby and walk the rest of the way.

I put the phone down. What did I think I was going to do? Rob the place?

A shiver flew over my skin. At first, I thought it was a shiver of distaste—but I realized, as I sank further into the fantasy of Wickham's unoccupied, treasure-filled home, that the shiver had been one of delicious anticipation.

I pulled the key out of my shirt and tapped it against my lips.

I needed money.

They had taken my money.

It was only right that I should have it back—by any means necessary.

But would it work? I'd been unable to take something as small as a chocolate pumpkin from Parallel 26. Given, I'd been trying to steal the *shadow* of a chocolate pumpkin.

I leaped up and hurried to the kitchen. I tucked the key under my shirt, against my skin, and then pulled a fork out of the drawer and held it tightly. "Calgon, take me away!"

The enchanted key apparently understood references to 1970s TV ads, because everything in my condo changed: the green velvet couch became gray, and the colorful mismatched dining chairs now mismatched in variations of gray. The noise of traffic in the streets below disappeared, replaced by a crystal-edged silence. Everything was calm, and cool, and lit with that same strange light.

Including the fork, which was still in my hand.

I walked slowly, out of the kitchen, across the living room, and down the hallway. I entered my bedroom, where framed photos of my smiling son somehow took on a reproachful look in black and white. I held the fork in one hand and pressed the other hand over my chest, where the key hung from its cord beneath my shirt. "I want to go back."

The bedspread filled with tones of blue, and the photos flushed with true color.

I still had the fork.

I'd been able to carry it from one side of the house to the other, through the black-and-white world, and bring it out into the real world.

Couldn't I do the same with anything I could carry from the Wickhams' home? I could sneak into the empty mansion safely, using the enchanted key, and take whatever I wanted by quickly slipping in and out of the real world.

Would they have left anything worth having behind? And did I have it in me to take whatever I wanted?

There was only one way to find out.

I went to my closet and rummaged around. "I'm just a little old lady out for an evening stroll. Well, hello, officer, how are you doing?" I pulled out a tunic-length navy turtleneck and a pair of dark gray leggings. Nighttime camouflage, but not conspicuously so. I only had white New Balance sneakers, so those would have to do. Gloves—I kept a pair deep in the closet for those rare cold days when I needed to wear them for driving until the car heater kicked in enough to take them off.

I stuffed the gloves in my purse and reached for my phone, intending to map out a route to a location near the island, but pulled back my hand. It might not be a good idea to leave a digital trail. I'd already looked up the house article and the address—that was bad enough. It would have to be good old-fashioned navigation by memory.

I couldn't bring my phone, either, since anybody looking at the cell phone tower pings could see I'd been on the island, if the worst happened and law enforcement got on my trail. I made double-sure I'd left it on the table before going out and locking the door behind me.

I drove out of the condo lot and turned east toward Miami Beach. Biscayne Bay glittered gold in the setting sun. I drove past the island, to a superstore about a quarter mile away on the Miami Beach peninsula. Plenty of parking, and not too far of a walk from Sun Island.

I pulled into a space in the back of the lot—less traffic, less chance of being seen. I hunched low over the passenger seat and, this time, I simply *thought* about going to the shadowy black-and-white world.

It worked.

When I sat up, the sky had gone from greenish-gold sunset to photo scrim white. The superstore's logo had changed from candy apple red to unassuming gray.

I got out of the car and left the parking lot on foot. All that walking I'd done back and forth to work was about to come in handy.

Like everywhere else in Miami, perfectly straight palm trees lined the sidewalks. The silence that had unnerved me at first now excited me, like being behind a theater curtain that was about to open. I trailed my fingers over a sidewalk-adjacent mural of monstera leaves before realizing that I didn't need to walk on the sidewalk at all.

With a laugh that came from nowhere, I skipped into the street.

A few steps more brought me back to the causeway I'd just driven over. Boats drifted in the still water of the bay. The island of palatial estates waited in the distance, a slim, artificial finger jutting into the water.

Although I'd crossed this particular causeway a hundred times—probably more—in a way it was like crossing it for the first time. Or like I was the first person to ever cross it at all. An inaugural crossing; a ribbon-cutting. "Look out, world. Here comes Lenore!"

One more small bridge, this one leading directly to the island.

The lonely security hut crouched empty before me. I couldn't help but laugh again. The grand mansions looked less like exclusive enclaves than great big treasure chests waiting to be opened. I didn't deviate from my destination, though—the Wickham residence or bust.

The ornate gates opened with the push of a finger.

I approached the double front door and almost knocked. I shook my head at my own impulse, then grasped the doorknob and turned it slowly, revealing the interior of the home.

The furniture had changed somewhat from the photos in the magazine feature, but it was the same in that it was still the wildly expensive type of furniture where if you had to ask the price, you couldn't afford it.

I sat in one of the strangely shaped side chairs and ran my hands over the cold leather. The art on the walls, so bright in the photos, looked flat and less impressive in black and white.

But I wasn't there for the art.

I got up from the fancy chair and headed upstairs, to the bedrooms.

When I opened the double doors to the suite at the top of the stairs, I gasped.

The chandelier over the bed probably cost as much as my car. Tiles of agate-like stone covered the walls. I approached the bed and touched the cover; the linen was so fine and so pure that it was practically its own light source.

Then I remembered the *zero zero zero* of my own retirement account—and my fingers curled like claws.

I left the bed in disgust and went to the figured wood dresser. It might have been cherry, but without color, I couldn't tell. I yanked out the top two drawers and scowled. "Underwear! Who wants your damn underwear. . ."

Then a small box of the same wood caught my eye; it had blended in, at first, on top of the dresser.

I picked it up and opened the lid. "Oh . . ."

Strands of thick metallic ropes lay within, as carelessly as plastic Mardi Gras beads littering the ground after a parade. Although they appeared silver, like everything else light-colored, I knew by feel they had to be gold. Silver never stayed that shiny. I drew them out, one after the other, and weighed them in my hands.

Together, the necklaces felt as weighty as the half pound of sliced Swiss cheese I bought on occasion at the grocery store. "Half a pound. . . let's see, that's eight ounces at—what is gold worth these days?" I hefted the necklaces again. "A lot, that's for sure."

Here, though, the necklaces were only a shadow of gold. Could I risk slipping into the real world to take the real thing?

On the other hand, could I risk *not* taking it? How else was I going to get by? Who would hire me at my age, and how likely was it not to be a job that would break down my body while starving my bank account?

Besides, who would it hurt? A rich bastard and his wife, who no doubt had a thousand, no, a *hundred* thousand times its value?

I replaced the jewelry and went to the luxuriously thick curtains by the window. I slipped behind the curtain—just in case someone had unexpectedly shown up while I was in the shadow world—and wished myself back to reality.

Ambient noises returned: first, the quiet marimba of bamboo stalks waving in the garden, followed by the coo of a mourning dove. No light came from the window; the sun had set completely.

My heart pounded. I peeked out from behind the curtain into the dark room.

I was alone.

I stepped out cautiously from behind the curtain and groped my way back to the dresser. My eyes didn't adjust to the dark as fast as they used to, and I had no flashlight to light my way. I'd have to bring one next time.

Next time. The thought gave me a thrill.

I opened the wooden box and scooped out the necklaces, clutching them all in one gloved hand.

I pressed my other hand over the key and pictured the shadow world, waiting for me on the other side like the turn of a page. No sooner had I pictured it than I was there, the white light sharp and cold.

I opened my hand and lifted a necklace from where it nestled in my palm.

I had brought it into the shadow world—but it was not *of* the shadow world. The necklace was gold, not the gold of the frame on the old condo lobby poster, or the gold of the buckle on my purse, but *real* gold.

And it was all mine.

8

I paused, irresolute, feeling my heart beat fast. The gold felt wonderfully heavy in my hands. Part of me wanted to ransack the place in search of more; part of me wanted to run home as fast as possible. What if the Wickhams returned from the Bahamas and I didn't get a chance to come back? Why leave money on the table—or wherever it might be hiding?

"Think, Lenore." I glanced around the sumptuous bedroom. "If you were a rich idiot, where would you leave your valuables?" Though the top two dresser drawers had held nothing of interest, that didn't mean there weren't other places to look.

I tucked the necklaces in my purse and carefully sank to my knees beside the bed. The cold gray light illuminated the space beneath the bed as well as it did everything else, revealing a small black duffle bag. I tugged it out and unzipped it—and clapped my gloved hands for joy.

They'd packed a go bag: a radio, a flashlight, batteries, a knife, some identity documents, first aid supplies, protein bars, medications, even some water purification tablets—and cash.

Lots of cash.

I reached in and pulled out a neatly bound packet. "Planning for when the revolution came?" I snorted. "You'd be first against the wall." Removing the cash revealed a soft velvet bag. I tugged at the drawstrings and upended it.

Bright, heavy coins spilled into my palm.

"Oh, you've got to be kidding me." Who was rich enough to leave this kind of money lying around while they jet off to the Bahamas?

CEOs who steal from their own employees, that's who.

Any hesitation I'd felt before disappeared like morning fog under the light of the sun. I pictured the real world and reappeared beside the bed, the room around me once again dark. I felt around beneath the bed and pulled out the bag I knew would be waiting there.

The go bag flashlight came in handy to see what I was doing as I methodically removed every packet of cash and every gold coin and placed them in my purse. I snagged a single protein bar for good measure. Then I packed everything else neatly back in its place, zipped the bag, and replaced it under the bed exactly as I'd found it.

In a fit of inspiration, I went to the dresser and placed one of the necklaces back in the box. With any luck, they'd think they had misplaced the others—what burglar would leave behind a solid gold necklace?—and they wouldn't check the go bag until it occurred to them to see if their ridiculous end-of-the-world protein bars expired.

I looked around the dark room one last time. I was a burglar, and I should have felt ashamed of myself—but I'd followed all the rules before, and look where it got me.

"To the shadows," I murmured, making the switch as easily as I would have pushed an elevator button.

I retraced my steps through the reflection of the house and emerged into the bleached light of the silver-white sky. The silent surroundings held no terror, not anymore—every house, every tree, every road was mine. I skipped a little as I crossed the island bridge, feeling younger than I had in years.

I returned to the superstore parking lot and got into my car. I hugged my purse to my chest and leaned down, out of sight, pressing myself as flat as possible before I made the switch to the real world. Instead of omnipresent white light, yellow parking lot lights made a feeble attempt at pushing back the darkness. I sat up slowly. The red logo beamed from the front of the store like an angry eye.

I was home.

I peeked into my purse. Cash and coins nestled safely in its depths. I removed my gloves, grabbed the protein bar, ripped the wrapper off, and devoured it. It didn't matter that it was made of some sort of awful protein paste—it tasted like misbehavior and victory. I hugged the purse once more, with feeling, and stashed it on the passenger seat before zipping downtown.

Normally, stepping out of my car at night would have put me on edge; as a woman, and an older woman at that, I couldn't be too careful. But with the knowledge that I could slide sideways into my own solitary pocket dimension, that fear evaporated. Who could mug me now? I could vanish like a wraith, and what would they do? Report a disappearing woman to the police? Hardly.

This revelation made my steps light all the way to my door.

Once inside, I set down my heavy purse and picked up my phone from where I'd left it on the table.

The notification light flashed.

I cringed. I'd missed my son's check-in call. The list of notifications showed he'd made a lot of them after I'd missed the first one.

I nearly mashed the call button in a panic, to reassure him, but then I lowered the phone. What would I tell him? Mom was off robbing houses? It would have to be something better than that, something reassuring and soothing and in line with the person he knew as his mother.

I lifted the phone and pressed the dial button.

"Mom? Where have you been? I've been calling and calling but you didn't pick up."

"I'm sorry—I fell asleep in front of the TV, and my ringer was off."

"Did you take your medicine?"

"Yes, of course." I scooted into the kitchen and retrieved the pill bottle from which, in fact, I had not yet taken my medication, silently swallowing the pill with a swig of water.

"You scared me."

"I'm fine. Go back to bed."

"It's only nine o'clock."

"Really?" It felt like I'd been out for hours. "I guess I lost track of time."

"That happens when you fall asleep," he said.

I chuckled. "Thanks for the tip. Love you, kiddo." I hung up and sighed. When had I become the child who needed to be checked on?

With that minor crisis averted, I emptied my purse on the coffee table. I put the gold coins in one stack, the cash in another, and the necklaces in a neat row. Seeing the haul in my very own home made it feel far more real than when I was at the Wickham house, or in the shadow world. No amount of *I'm a harmless old lady* charm would excuse a pile of stolen goods on my coffee table.

That made hiding it my first priority.

Could I put it in the shadow world? And if I did, would it be there when I came back?

I'd have to test it before I trusted it. I went to my closet and pulled out a rainbow-colored silk scarf, easy to spot in a monochromatic setting. I concentrated on the black-and-white version of my condo, and the real world flipped away before my eyes. My condo looked rather severe in shades of gray.

Where to put the scarf, though? I didn't need to hide it, so I simply placed it on the dining table where it would be clearly in view when I came back—if it was still there.

I wished myself back to the real world and returned to sit in front of my treasure pile.

Since the shadow world wasn't a solution for the moment, I'd have to come up with an alternate safe location to store the cash and gold. Banks were out—I didn't need cameras and paperwork to document my every move. Where in the real world could I put the stash?

And then it hit me—*Black Mangrove Preserve.*

I could walk in, wait for a quiet moment to disappear, and then continue walking through the woods on the shadow side. No bugs, no people, and most importantly—no trail to be followed. I'd simply return to the real world long enough to bury the treasure before disappearing and retracing my steps. Everything would be safe, off the beaten trail, waiting for me to dig it up whenever I needed it.

I tipped my head back against the couch and smiled.

9

As soon as Parallel 26 opened the next morning, I was through the door, across the floor, and at the rack with the swing coat in my hands. It was just as buttery soft as I remembered. I carefully removed it from the hanger and draped it over my shoulders. I turned this way and that in front of a nearby mirror, admiring the free and easy motion of the cape.

A young woman dressed in something trendy appeared over my shoulder. "Can I help you?"

Our eyes met in the mirror. Her expression had a kind of challenge in it, but I was too happy with the coat to pay too much attention. "I don't think so."

"Are you looking for something for your daughter?"

I froze with my fingers wrapped around the luxurious lapels. "Excuse me?"

"For your *daughter*," she repeated, as if I were hard of hearing.

My hands went to my sides and balled into fists. "What makes you think I was shopping for my daughter when I was clearly *standing in front of a mirror* trying on something for myself?"

Her mouth opened and closed.

I shrugged off the jacket as fast as I could. "Here." I handed it to her. "You can keep it. Maybe you'll find someone young enough to sell it to."

I stormed out, my good mood vaporized. It didn't help that I caught another glimpse of my roots as I passed the shop window. Why couldn't I just be what I was? Old, young—who cared?

In my frazzled state I'd walked the wrong direction and ended up in front of one of the downtown hotels, this one with a hair salon situated in the front of the glassed-in lobby. I'd almost turned on my heel when I caught a glimpse of one of the hairdressers through the window.

She was about my age, with an exceptionally black braid pulled over her shoulder—and a stunning streak of white that rose from her crown like a flame.

I nearly pressed my nose against the window like a kid at a candy store. "I'm in love," I said, my voice tinged with desire. I pushed open the door. "Excuse me"—I pointed to the woman's hair—"Is that something you can do for me?"

Her hands went to her hairline. "The white streak?" She smiled and came out from behind the desk. "I think it would look stunning on you."

I clasped my hands together. "Can you fit me in? Please fit me in."

"As it so happens, I have a cancellation this morning—"

"Yes! Let's go."

She laughed and led the way.

The shampoo washed away the old Lenore, the one who plodded through life, doing everything she was supposed to do, and got screwed over for it.

Old Lenore swirled away down the drain with the suds.

New Lenore sat up with a towel around her shoulders, dripping water and ready to take on the world.

When it was done, the stylist handed me a mirror so I could see my hair from every angle. She'd performed some kind of magic that gave my plain brown hair a subtle multicolored dimension. The white streak shot upward at just the right angle and width, looking bold and new against the rest of my hair. "You're an artist," I sighed.

She whipped away the cape. "I only revealed what was already there."

After paying the bill, I dug in my purse for a healthy tip—courtesy of the Wickhams—and pressed it into her hands. "Thank you."

The day was still young and I had so much to do.

Part of my problem, I realized, was that I hadn't been thinking big enough. Stealing table scraps from the Wickhams was fun, but it was small change—and while their small change could make up for my own personal shortfall temporarily, it didn't cover the long term.

I needed some way to get all that money back; or, failing that, something that would send the Elozent executives to jail for a good, long time.

But before I could figure all that out, I needed to do something about all the cash and gold I had sitting around.

The cash was easy enough—I had to hide it, like I'd planned—but the gold needed to be converted to cash.

I strolled past Parallel 26 on my way home. The jacket I'd wanted still hung in the window display, but for some reason, its hold on me was gone. I could have stolen it, if I wanted to, but I didn't even want it anymore. Instead, as I glanced at my blue linen blouse and white slacks, I felt an urge to change into something tougher.

I had an idea of where I could kill two birds with one stone.

I returned to my condo and pulled out my old toolbox. I rummaged around until I found a pair of sharp wire cutters.

I retrieved the gold necklaces. I picked one up, unclasped it, and draped it loosely around one wrist, eyeballing the length. Then I snipped the chain into bracelet-length pieces.

I held the cut chains and admired my handiwork. "Voilà. From stolen necklace to random broken bracelets."

Then, I split the cash into a smaller amount for my wallet and a larger bundle to be hidden in the woods. I bagged the remaining necklaces and the large cash bundle, and stowed them in my purse.

I drove out of the city and headed for the seven-day-a-week flea market on the outskirts of town.

From the outside, it didn't look like much: no carefully tended landscaping, no ornamental palm trees. Just a flat black asphalt parking lot in front of a row of rickety-looking buildings fronted by blindingly-colored signs advertising a "SALE!" that never ended.

The main building boasted a display of vintage cars parked like toy vehicles in the center of a dilapidated food court. A large metal chicken statue stood watch over the tables—and if that didn't get your appetite going, you could take the neon-lit stairs to the second floor gallery to shop for knockoff cologne, Halloween costumes, and leopard-print furniture.

I crossed the checkerboard floor to reach the more far-flung booths outside the main building.

The heavy, sweet scent of fruit filled the air when I exited the main building—but I wasn't there for the produce.

I was there for the shopkeepers who didn't ask too many questions.

A pink neon "JEWELRY–PAWN–CASH" sign glowed in the distance down the aisle. Very straightforward. I patted my hair and straightened my blouse as I approached.

The shop proprietor—a bearded young man in well-worn cargo pants, army green t-shirt, and a camouflage ball cap—stood behind a row of fluorescent-lit jewelry cases. Behind him, rows of beat-up shelves held an assortment of electronic devices.

I pretended to look in the case while I worked up some courage. Finally, I took a deep breath, reaching for the right combination of self-assured and wholly innocent. "Excuse me."

He looked up from his phone.

"Do you buy broken gold?"

Without speaking, he retrieved a small scale and some sort of black rectangular stone and laid them on the display case. He leaned on the case and looked at me with a bored expression.

I got the hint. I dug the "broken" bracelets out of my purse and laid them on the glass.

He picked them up and rubbed each one against the black stone, where they left visible marks. Then he moved the gold to the scale. "One thousand."

"Dollars?"

He nodded.

"Okay."

He swept the chains off the case and out of sight, then pulled a massive wad of cash from his pocket. He peeled off ten hundred-dollar bills and handed them to me, then tucked the wad back in his pocket and returned to staring at his phone.

I stood there with the cash in my hands. It seemed almost too easy. "No—uh—paperwork, or anything?"

He spared me a glance that said: *Are you kidding?*

I stuffed the cash in my purse. "Hey, you look like an outdoor kind of fella." I gestured to his hat. "You know someplace around here I can get some clothes like that?" If I was going to make it a habit to walk in the woods, I needed sturdier clothes.

"Aisle sixteen," he said, without bothering to look up from his phone.

The maze of booths seemed to have no order whatsoever. I passed tables filled with flats of strawberries followed by bookshelves crammed with used books, followed by a booth that appeared to sell only belts and oversized belt buckles, before I found the right stall.

The clothes weren't fancy, but the price was right. I picked up some ripstop cargo pants and a water-resistant jacket with hidden pockets.

I paid with cash and took away my items in a wrinkled plastic grocery bag.

On the way out, I stopped at one of the produce stands to reward myself with a freshly-squeezed lemonade. The citrus press crushed the juice out each lemon half, and the empty shells made a hollow thump as they dropped into the trash can.

I took the cold plastic cup and sipped.

When life gives you lemons . . .

You smash every last drop from the damn things.

10

The Elozent Industries building cast a shadow over the plaza. The prism-like "E" sculpture split the sunlight into rainbow shards that flickered onto the surrounding ligustrum hedges. The black plinth beneath the sculpture looked severe and flat, like a sacrificial altar.

The brass-handled front doors beckoned.

I crossed the plaza and entered with what I hoped looked like a swagger of confidence.

I didn't get ten steps in before the security guard stopped me. "Ma'am, may I see your badge?"

"My badge?" I patted my pockets. "I must have left it at home."

He must have felt some sympathy, because he reached for the phone. "Is there someone I can call for authorization?"

"Authorization?" I blinked. "You need authorization for me to get my shoes?"

He looked at me like I'd lost my marbles. "Your shoes?"

I popped my foot to display a sneaker. "I left my heels under my desk on the last day, before they locked everything up."

He raised an eyebrow. "Ma'am, we're not allowed to let anyone go up there unaccompanied right now."

I could tell he was wavering, so I leaned into my harmless-old-lady advantage. "Please? Maybe someone could come up with me? I promise I won't be a moment." Was I batting my eyelashes too much?

He released a heavy sigh and called to another guard across the lobby. "Watch the doors for a minute, will you?" He gestured for me to precede him to the elevators.

We stepped into the elevator.

He inserted a key into the button panel. "What floor?"

"Thirty."

The Muzak played over the awkward silence as the elevator surged upward. When we reached my floor, the bell dinged and the doors slid open. We stepped out.

I surveyed the mess of papers and paper shreds. "Wow, no one's been up here to clean, have they?"

He wasn't the chatty type—obviously—but he shook his head.

I threaded my way between the desks until I reached my old desk, looking forlorn with its sad garland of disconnected wires. I stooped carefully and snagged my pumps from under the desk.

The problem was, I didn't want to leave just yet.

I needed to take down the executives for real—but to do that, I needed something to take them down *with*.

Surely there was something on the executive floor that would prove they'd planned all this. A smoking gun. They wouldn't have been shredding paper by the pound if there wasn't some kind of evidence hidden in there—but the guard was clearly anxious to get going.

How could I get up there?

"Hey, my boss asked me to grab something he left in his office on the next floor. You mind if I pop up there for a second?"

This time, the guard's eyebrows didn't rise. He wasn't even considering the idea of letting me go. "Can't. Nobody's allowed up there."

I exhaled my disappointment. I'd gotten as far as I could get, and it was clear I couldn't haul out mounds of paper on his watch, so I tucked my shoes under my arm and walked back to the elevator.

The ride down was just as awkward as the ride up.

I thanked him on the way out, and got a light grunt in return.

Outside, I sat heavily on the edge of one of the planters. It hadn't gone great, but what had I expected? The building was still locked up tight. They weren't letting anyone in while the creditors fought over what was left.

My gaze traveled up, up, up the side of the building, all the way to the observation deck, which was so high it looked much smaller than it really was. Could I get up there? And if I could, would I be able to find something that would implicate the executives?

Sneaking through the shadows would get me around any ground floor guards. But without an elevator, I'd never make it to the executive floor—not thirty-one floors high.

It wasn't like I could fly.

Or could I?

The key, which had lain quietly against my skin for some time, suddenly warmed.

"I'm not a witch," I said to myself.

The key pulsed again, almost encouragingly.

"Even if I know where the witches are, they won't help me."

ZAP.

"Ow! Lay off."

The key settled into a dissatisfied hum.

Every city had its own spot where witches gravitated. Back home, in Sparkle Beach, it used to be an abandoned factory building where she—*they*—could practice in secret. Of course, I wasn't allowed to come along.

I used to sneak in and watch anyway. Good thing I paid close attention when they gossiped about witches in other cities—and their hangouts.

In Miami, a bigger city with far more witches than Sparkle Beach, the gathering place was more like a private speakeasy. And to get in, you had to prove you had magic.

I didn't have elemental magic. That was obvious.

But could I bluff my way past?

Like any good speakeasy, Magic City Tiki only opened at night.

I checked my appearance in the mirror and touched the streak in my hair. I didn't like wearing my hair loose. I almost always wore it up in a chignon or twist unless I was sleeping. But the evening seemed to call for something more unique, so I created a long braid and pinned it up like a crown. The braid made a nice underscore to the white blaze rising from my hairline.

Magic City Tiki sat hidden in the backstreets of one of the local artsy neighborhoods, the kind with murals on every wall and art installations around every corner. The streetlights washed everything with a yellow glow, including a metal statue of a sea creature with a scaled dragon's tail and a grinning horse's skull head. The shifting shadows made it look like it might spring to life at any moment.

The entrance to Magic City Tiki was unmarked. If you didn't know where the red door with ornamental hinges led, you'd keep on walking to one of the more attractive hangouts.

I knocked on the door.

It creaked open to reveal a man wearing a Cuban-style shirt and a Panama hat. He leaned on the doorframe and looked me up and down with casual appraisal. "You looking for something?"

"I'd like a drink."

"This is a private party, love."

"I have an invitation."

He made a beckoning motion with one hand and stepped back, into the darkness.

I crossed the threshold.

He shut the door behind me, blocking out the last gasp of illumination from the streetlights.

Afterimages obscured my vision until my eyes adjusted.

A second door stood opposite of my position.

The doorman had taken a seat on a lone barstool next to a small table holding a lit candle, a potted plant, and a bowl of water. "Go ahead, love."

I hesitated. I'd never used the key in front of someone—not intentionally, anyway. It felt like giving up a powerful secret.

He watched me with a neutral expression. "You nervous?"

I laughed, shakily. "A little."

"Don't worry. Everyone is nervous the first time."

"How do you know this is my first time?"

He just smiled.

I pictured the other world, black and white and cool, a silent mirror reflection of reality—and I was there. Soft white light lit the room in shades of gray. The candle, the plant, and the bowl had become a monochromatic still life. The doorman was gone, and the fire had gone out.

I counted to ten. That should have been a long enough disappearance to prove my "power," so I concentrated on returning to the real world.

The doorman observed my reappearance without startling in the slightest. He tilted his head. "Very nice. I don't think I've ever seen anything like that. Are you an air witch?"

"Mm-hm," I said, hoping he wouldn't have any more questions.

He reached for my hand and traced his finger over the back of it like someone writing down a phone number. "This will last for tonight. You'll need a new one next time, okay?"

I lifted my hand and admired the back of it as if I were wearing a new ring. "Thank you." I couldn't see a thing. Presumably, he'd traced something in magic.

He got up and opened the far door. "Have fun."

Music pulsed from the room beyond, and red light spilled through the doorframe.

I entered the witches' speakeasy.

11

onga drumbeats measured my footsteps, and the high panpipe-like voice of Yma Sumac trilled over the rhythm. Low tables surrounded by dark wooden nautical chairs lined the walls of the intimate room. Niches punctuated the walls. Each niche held a tiki statue: this one holding a real flame, that one topped with a bonsai coming out of its head, another with a waterfall spilling from its mouth. I looked around for a fourth—but when I found it, it wasn't in a niche at all.

The fourth tiki was mounted to the ceiling and surrounded by stylized wooden leaves that spun at a stately pace.

I was gawking at the tiki fan, and it wasn't a good look for fitting in, so I crossed to the far end of the windowless room and took a seat at the bar. The bar itself held kitschy tiki glasses and criss-crossed strands of colorful lights, plus an actual carved pumpkin lit from within by a real fire. The whole array wouldn't have looked out of place in your average Miami tourist spot—except the bartender set the drink she was preparing on fire just by snapping her fingers.

I jumped, but not because of the fire.

Because of the memories.

The bartender placed the drink on a cocktail napkin and delivered it to a witch at the shadowy end of the bar, then returned. "What'll it be?"

"Virgin mojito." I'd promised myself to keep a clear head no matter what.

While she prepared my drink, I swiveled around to take another look at the crowd. Some witches laughed, others canoodled. Fire and water witches were easy to spot. They couldn't resist playing with their own powers. One obvious water witch funnelled her drink through midair rather than through a straw. The liquid caught the red glare from the lights.

But air witches . . . they weren't as obvious.

"Looking for someone?" asked the bartender.

I swung back around. "Maybe."

She handed me the mojito.

I took the tall, cold glass. It was risky to just *ask* for help—I certainly didn't want any questions in return—but there was no other way to see if someone could help me get to the observation deck on the Elozent tower. I cleared my throat and addressed the bartender. "Know any air witches looking for work?"

"What kind of work?"

"Paid work."

She polished a glass thoughtfully. "Not too many witches who work for hire."

I suppressed the urge to roll my eyes. Of course not. They were far above all that. It was considered tacky. "Are you sure there's no one?"

The bartender set down the glass. "Maybe Sondra."

"Sondra?"

She jerked her head. "Down at the end of the bar."

A puff of vapor cloaked the woman at the end of the bar, making it impossible to see her face.

I collected my drink and moved to a barstool next to her. The cloud cleared.

Sondra waved her long fingers over the flaming drink and the fire extinguished. She took a delicate sip, set the glass down, and raised some kind of small cartridge to her lips. She exhaled another cloud.

It dissipated around wild curls piled like a bird's nest on her head.

"Excuse me," I said.

She gave no indication that she'd heard me.

"I was told you might be interested in some work. Are you an air witch?"

The cloud drifted toward me. It collapsed into a miniature rain cloud over my mojito. Miniscule raindrops plinked on the ice. Then, the cloud dissolved in a rapid puff of air. "Does that answer your question?" she said.

"One of them."

"What kind of work?"

"I need to fly."

Sondra chuckled to herself.

"What's so funny?"

"Because that is a very difficult request." Her gaze slid over and met mine. She looked amused—and crafty. "Don't you *know* any air witches?"

"Let's say I'm not from around here."

Sondra tilted her head philosophically. "We could say that, but would it be true?" She drank, more deeply this time, and set the glass on its napkin. "What kind of witch did you say you were?"

My stomach trembled. "I didn't."

She waited for me to continue, but when I didn't, she gave an elegant shrug. "It's a small community, here in Miami. Most of us know each other." The look she gave me was pointed, as in *I don't know you*. "You probably won't find what you need that way."

"Oh? Is there another way?"

"Depends."

"On what?"

"On how much it's worth to you."

"What would you say is reasonable?"

Her eyes narrowed. "Let's say . . . five hundred dollars."

I laughed. "Five hundred dollars? For what? You said it was too difficult."

"Too difficult for most air witches, yes." She leaned in. "But not too difficult, perhaps, to give you information you can use."

Adrenalin shot through me. "What do you mean?"

She looked at me expectantly.

I hesitated, then fished in my purse for the cash I'd received at the flea market. I folded up five hundred-dollar bills and passed them to her under the bar.

She tucked them away. "There's an art exhibit at the Hibiscus—the big museum on the bay?"

"Yeah, sure, but—"

She waved a long finger to silence me. "Featuring magical objects." She leaned a little closer. "One of the objects is real."

"Real magic?"

She nodded.

"Air magic?"

"Air magic. And more."

"How do I know you're telling the truth?"

"You don't."

Even though the mojito was nonalcoholic, I felt tipsy. I had to lean on the bar. "Which of the objects is real?"

She pinched the tips of her thumb and index fingers together, making a shape like a pointed oval. She lifted her hand and peered at me through the oval. "The one that looks like an eye."

"Why are you telling me this?"

She lowered her hand. "Do you know whose collection is on loan for the exhibit?"

"No . . ."

"The Elozent people. You know—Robert Wickham." She paused. "And his wife." Her face took on a strange expression, as if the last word had tasted funny.

My eyes widened. "Do the Wickhams know what they own?"

Sondra looked away and waved a hand. "Why would they? They're not witches; they're vultures." She took a long pull from her cartridge and blew an angry puff. "Buying treasures with money they stole from everyone else."

We sat in silence, each of us presumably contemplating how much we hated the Wickhams.

I caught her gaze again. "You won't . . . *say* anything about this?"

"Why would I? If you can take it, you're doing me a favor. Anything that annoys Robert Wickham is fine by me." Sondra seemed to fold in on herself, cutting off contact as if I no longer existed. Loose curls fell forward like curtains. She blew another vaporous cloud and was lost to sight.

I left some bills next to my unfinished drink and slid off the barstool.

The tiki fire still burned merrily, flickering in the slow breeze from the tiki fan. I wanted to linger in the witches' hideaway. I could stay and pretend to be one of them, drinking one virgin mojito after another, until last call. But how long before I was revealed as an imposter? How long before they saw me for what I truly was? Even Sondra seemed to suspect something, and that was only after speaking to her for a few moments.

It was clear I couldn't pass for long enough to stay and enjoy myself, so I left the same way I'd come. I passed the tables surrounded by convivial witches and reentered the first room. I crossed it before the doorman could say a word, so eager was I to be gone—but at the threshold to the street, I turned around for one last look before the inner door swung closed.

The red glow vanished and Yma Sumac's high note was cut off mid-vocalization; the doorman was left sitting in the near-darkness. His voice reached me like a benediction: "Have a good night, love."

I nodded, though he probably could see me only in silhouette. "I will."

12

The next morning, I returned to Black Mangrove Preserve with the remaining gold and excess cash. Dark clouds boiled through the sky. I wore my new water-resistant jacket and a new pair of boots that would hold up better than my usual white sneakers.

The elevated walkway wound through cypress trees and palmettos, over swampy terrain and islands of grass. By the time I'd gone a half mile, I was sure there was no one to see me. The threat of rain had chased away casual visitors.

I stopped on a part of the walkway that curved over a stretch of dry land. The flat, grassy area stretched into the distance, ending at a lightning-blasted tree—a natural landmark. All I needed to do was get down to the ground, switch over to the black-and-white world, and make my way through the tall grass to the tree.

The walkway was close enough to the ground at that point where I could have easily sat on the edge of the planks and scooted down. Unfortunately, the double guardrail timbers were too close to get between. Instead, I had to go over the railing and down the side. It was a task that was probably better suited to a younger Lenore, but I managed to make it down without breaking my neck.

I ducked down into the grass beneath the walkway and imagined the expansive field before me in shades of gray. I made the switch—and not a moment too soon. The real grass was probably filled with snakes and God knew what else.

I tugged my jacket into place and started walking. There was no sound but my footsteps and the soft white noise of my body parting the sea of gray grass one step at a time.

By the time I reached the gnarled old tree, I was sweating. I made my way around the black trunk, to the far side, where—if I hunched down—I couldn't be seen from the walkway.

"To the real world," I said.

The grass turned green and brown, but the tree was almost the exact same shade of black as it had been in the shadow world.

I wiped my brow and set my purse on an exposed tree root. I pulled out a shiny new gardening spade and set to work digging a hole at the base of the trunk. The triple-bagged gold and cash made a clinking thump when it landed in the dirt. Having no desire to meet the local snake population—or get struck by lightning—I filled in the hole, smoothed the dirt, and hurriedly made the switch to the other world.

The soothing white sky brought a sigh of relief to my lips. The great outdoors wasn't so bad when it was climate-controlled and devoid of creepy, crawling life. I pushed my way through the grass again, all the way back to the walkway. There was no way to know for sure if anyone was in sight on the other side. If anyone happened to see me emerge from the tall grass, I'd say I dropped something over the side of the walkway by accident, and had to climb down to get it.

With that alibi in mind, I made the final switch—back to the real world, with plenty of motivation to get up and out of the grass before Mr. Snakey decided to pay me a visit. The climb up was much harder than the climb down, and by the time I was standing on the walkway again, a nap seemed like the obvious next step.

Rain pattered on the walkway. I pulled up my hood and headed for the trail entrance.

When I exited the walkway and entered the clearing, I heard someone shout.

"Hey!"

I froze. That voice was familiar . . .

"Mom!"

Oh. That was why it was familiar. I slowly pivoted in my son's direction and pasted on a carefree smile. "Sheridan! What are you doing here? I thought you weren't coming here again until the Trail or Treat." In fact, I'd been counting on it.

He zipped up his own water-resistant jacket with the official park service logo on it. "They needed somebody to liaise with the university students today." He looked me up and down, then lightly tugged at the hood on my jacket. "Since when did you start shopping at the army surplus store?"

I pulled my head back with a light laugh. Droplets of water snuck beneath my hood and trickled down my forehead like sweat. "I'm just doing what you told me to do—get some fresh air, remember?"

His gaze shifted to my sturdy outdoor boots. "I don't think I pictured you going all Grizzly Adams on me."

"My beard isn't full enough for that."

He laughed. "What say we get out of this drizzle and you tell me what else you've been up to?"

That didn't sound like a good idea at all. "Oh, I really should get going."

"Mom, you're retired—where else do you have to be?"

I gasped in mock horror. "Shame on you, Sheridan Frost. As if just because I was retired meant I had nowhere to be. For all you know, I have a hot date."

He looked simultaneously shocked and curious. "Do you?"

I kept a poker face for one beat longer, then laughed. "No."

He smirked. "Neither do I. I can't judge."

I hugged him, wet jacket and all. "How about we catch up this weekend?" By then, I could come up with a plausible cover story for whatever I was actually doing. I released him but held on to him at arm's length. "All right?"

He studied my face like he was trying to identify animal tracks. Then his eyes narrowed. "You're not telling me something."

I let go of him and turned to walk before he could get a better look at my reaction. "Nonsense."

He caught up. "Fine. The weekend. You can come help me at the Trail or Treat. And—"

"Don't forget to take my medication, yes, I know." I kept walking, but faster.

"Love you!" he called.

I waved over my shoulder without looking back. Part of what I had said was true. I did have things to do—like figuring out how to steal the mysterious magic eye from the Hibiscus Museum.

I drove back downtown. Instead of going directly to the Hibiscus, I left my car at the condo tower and walked to the public library.

Thankfully, the sea breeze had pushed the rain inland.

I wasn't ready to get caught on camera at the museum—not yet, anyway—and the library computers were more anonymous than using my own phone to dig for information.

The cream-colored, terracotta-roofed building faced an expansive courtyard. Roman arches made up an entire side of the building; I passed under one of them to enter. Inside, a similar pattern continued: arches everywhere, and the same beige color as the exterior walls.

I used a fake name—*Blanche Devereaux*—to sign up for an hour of computer time.

I navigated to the museum website, like any tourist might, and found the exhibition featured prominently on the front page.

Magic: Art and Artifacts Across the Ages. Sponsored by Elozent, on loan from the personal collection of Robert and Jane Wickham.

There were other sponsors, of course, but Elozent and the Wickhams got top billing and a bigger font than anyone else. They must have arranged the sponsorship long before the company went under, of course.

I compared a wide shot photograph of the gallery space to the downloadable exhibition map. It appeared that the object Sondra had mentioned had its own display plinth in the center, and an actual title: *The Eye of the Elements*.

The major problem would be that I couldn't steal the Eye while in the shadows. I'd have to steal it in real life, then make my escape. The museum's security cameras would capture every moment of the theft, even if I could sneak up under the cover of the shadow world. No matter how fast I could lift the cover, grab the Eye, and disappear, I would leave behind a dangerous amount of video evidence.

What to do?

I leaned back in the uncomfortably hard chair and considered my options. One: I could give up.

Not an option.

Two: I could try to disguise myself.

Maybe. But what possible disguise would conceal my body type, height, hair color, and age all at once?

Three: I could give it some time and try to come up with a better plan.

No, I didn't want to wait. I wanted it *now*. I could already feel its oval contours in my palm.

The key, in its hidden spot beneath my shirt, radiated a tiny burst of heat as warm as the air above birthday candles. The sensation startled me. My hand jogged, and I accidentally clicked the menu above the exhibition page.

The museum events page appeared.

"Events?" I muttered. "What do I need with events?" I was about to click away when I saw the next upcoming event on the calendar.

October 28th – Halloween Gala.

I peered at the description.

An enchanted evening of light bites and sips. Costumes highly suggested! Show us your best and baddest witch hats, brooms, robes, capes, and wands. Buy your tickets now; this event will sell out.

A crowded event with everyone in witch hats and witchy clothing?

The smile that spread over my face felt wicked.

I had my solution.

13

The museum rose like a glass Rubik's cube behind pillars covered in thick green leafy vines. Tall vertical planters hung like stalactites from a lattice of steel beams extending outward from the museum walls; in the fading light, the pillars and hanging planters gave the impression of a mouth with very long green teeth.

I tugged the brim of my witch hat lower and joined the line at the entrance. A hand-written sign was taped to the door: *No Brooms Allowed*. I hadn't brought one.

I needed my hands free.

As I had planned, my own costume blended well with the crowd. Although the predominant costume color was black, jewel tone accents turned up on hatbands, corsets, vests, and cape linings. In a perfect world, everyone would have been completely interchangeable—the better to be anonymous—but this was as close as it would get.

I handed over my ticket and entered the building.

The usual white lights had been exchanged for a moody purple, and the Eagles' "Witchy Woman" blasted over the sound system. Several people in the lobby—obviously a few drinks deep—burst into song on the chorus.

I ignored the table of tiny appetizer bites and passed a champagne fountain before entering the exhibition hall.

The first exhibit contained a long row of brooms arranged in order from newest to oldest, starting with a modern yellow-handled broom. They got more interesting down the row, moving from flat to round, and from plastic to wood. Some of the antique brooms had handles made from bronze or silver; others had bits of velvet trim.

Further in, there were cases filled with tiny gold masks and intricately carved figurines. Another wall held an assortment of hand-woven hangings. I gave them all a cursory glance, like a typical partygoer, and kept moving.

Then, I saw it.

Small enough to fit comfortably in my palm, and lit by a spotlight that made it seem to wink when it glittered, the Eye sat alone on its plinth, in a shaped nest of burgundy velvet, with a clear plastic display cube over the top. The glossy inlays fit neatly together to form the shape of a multicolored iris around a silver pupil. Intricate silver filigree wrapped the edges.

I wanted to keep staring, but I couldn't afford to—there were cameras everywhere, and I didn't want to stand out on the surveillance footage. Instead, I moved on to the auditorium, where the costume contest would be held. Though the doors had only recently opened, the signup list already ran to over a hundred names.

If that trend continued, the galleries would be nearly empty during the contest.

I left the auditorium and entered the women's restroom off the main gallery. It was fancy enough to have a lounge in addition to the usual facilities. Modernist furniture filled the lounge space, and a row of mirrors lined the far wall above a stone countertop. People had discarded hats and other accessories before entering the restroom area—presumably to avoid costume difficulties in the stalls.

My black witch hat still completely obscured my hair, but I pulled it down again just to make sure it stayed in place. My plain black cape covered an equally plain black dress underneath. Nothing to stand out, nothing to be noticed.

Just another old lady in a witch costume.

A young woman in a rainbow-colored fortune-teller's costume appeared at my shoulder. She picked up a glittery mask from the countertop and settled it over her face, then gave me a thumbs-up. "Nice crone costume!" She glided away out of the lounge.

I looked at myself in the mirror again. A crone?

Maybe.

But I was about to be a very powerful one. I allowed myself a witchy smile before exiting to the gallery.

Killing time never felt so painful. I lingered at every display but the one I really wanted to look at. I carried around a glass of champagne, pretending to sip. I ate stale, unidentifiable appetizer bites in tiny phyllo cups. I shadowed larger groups so I didn't stand out as being alone at the party.

Finally—finally!—a docent announced the beginning of the costume contest. People moved in the direction of the auditorium like little schools of fish.

Except for one man who made a beeline toward me.

The weird purple light made it hard to distinguish his face. He wore what looked like a graduation robe over shirt and slacks, and a wizard hat that could have doubled for a dunce cap.

Whoever he was, I didn't have time for it. I turned on my heel and started walking.

"Lenore!"

I stopped short and squeezed my eyes shut. Surely, it couldn't be—

"It's me, Mauricio!"

I slowly turned. Of course. He hadn't had to miss his Halloween party after all.

"Guess what? I got a new job!" He clapped his hand on my shoulder.

I slid out from under it. "That's wonderful, really it is, but—"

"So what have you been up to?"

"Well, actually—" I looked around for a way out and spotted the sign for the women's restroom. "I was just about to visit the little girls' room, if you know what I mean." It did not escape me that this was the second time I'd used this excuse in the last week.

"Oh!" His eyes widened. "Don't let me stop you. See you at the costume contest!" He raised his glass.

"Sure thing," I said, already starting to sidle away.

When he turned toward the auditorium, I hurried to the women's restroom.

The lounge countertop held a new assortment of items: a black hat just like mine—no, that wouldn't do—and a purple hat—perfect—a long red cloak, and a cat mask.

No one else was in the lounge.

I grabbed the purple hat, the red cloak, and the mask, and stuffed them under my black cape. Sweat broke out on my brow. I hurried into an open stall, then shut and locked the door.

My heart pounded.

Could I do this?

I pictured the Eye, waiting for me—*winking* at me—in the gallery. The key, hidden beneath my witch costume, resting against my chest, felt calm and cool.

Yes. Yes, I could.

I took a slow breath and blew it out. I made sure I had a firm grasp on the accessories I'd swiped from the lounge. I pictured the museum in black and white, and made the switch to the shadow world.

The cold whitish-gray light was a balm in contrast to the noise and garish purple lighting of the party. I rested my forehead against the wall of the stall and gathered myself.

I could still turn back. I'd only taken a few bits of clothing, easily returned. Mauricio had seen me—could identify me—but so what? My presence didn't mean I'd be a suspect. A woman in her sixties, robbing museums in a witch costume? It was too silly to imagine.

The truth was: I didn't want to turn back. Not when I'd come this far, when I was *so close* to getting the magic that should have been mine all along.

As calming as the gray silence was, I couldn't stay in the bathroom stall forever. I had to get moving. The door was already unlatched, so I pulled it open and faced my black-and-white reflection in the mirror over the bathroom sink.

I pulled the purple hat and red cloak from under my cape. In my hands, they had color; in the mirror, they had none. I removed my hat and affixed the cat mask with its elastic band. I traded my black cape for the red one, then topped everything off with the purple hat.

If they looked for the thief, they'd be looking for someone who'd been wearing a purple hat, a red cape, and a cat mask—and that person would not exist.

I passed the lounge and reentered the gallery, now empty and quiet and monochrome.

The Eye glittered on its plinth.

I approached.

The inset gems looked more severe in black and white, and the label squared neatly with the corner of the plinth. *The Eye of the Elements, early 20th century, United States. Believed to be an amulet in the Greek apotropaic style commonly known as the "evil eye." The amulet is intended to deflect misfortune by calling upon the classical elements of earth, air, fire, and water.*

I lifted the clear cube experimentally. It came free without effort. There wasn't a locking mechanism—it was just a cover.

My breath released as a happy sigh. I let the cube slip back into place.

I could have appeared out of thin air right next to the display, but I didn't know what would happen if I materialized on top of someone, and I didn't want to find out the hard way. Instead, I retreated to an empty corner of the gallery and faced outward. I retrieved my gloves from my pocket and slipped them on.

I placed one hand over my heart, as much to calm the racing beats as to feel the outline of the key beneath my clothes, and reentered the real world.

14

The gallery was almost empty. A few partygoers lingered by the brooms, but the plinth was clear.

I quick-marched to the Eye. My gloved hands went to the sides of the cube—flat, palms facing in, like you might put your hands on the cheeks of someone you loved. I lifted the cover off and set it down on the floor. I seized the Eye and tucked it in my pocket, then replaced the cube on the empty display. If it bought a few more seconds before anyone realized something was amiss, so much the better. Lucky for me, no alarms had even gone off yet.

I returned to the shadow world in an instant. The plinth stood as empty here as it did in the real world. My hands shook as I pulled off the mask and drew off my gloves. I shoved my hand into my pocket. My fingers closed around the Eye. I drew it out cautiously, as if it might go off at any moment.

I held the Eye in one hand and lifted my other hand. "Wind," I commanded.

Nothing happened.

Had the witch lied to me?

Should I put it back and run?

No, she hadn't been lying. I saw the truth on her face when she mentioned Elozent and the Wickhams.

I just didn't know what I was doing. Yet.

I pocketed the Eye and made for the exit.

The empty nighttime Miami streets didn't worry me in this quiet alternate reality. The waterfront path outside the museum led me south on a wide promenade along the bay. A right-hand turn took me into the downtown business district. I discarded the cat mask and threw off the red cape and the purple hat—better for them to stay in the shadow world, like my original black cape and hat. The black dress I likewise discarded. The change left me in leggings and a light-weight top, suitable for walking the downtown streets without attracting attention.

I found an alley, pressed myself into a corner, and returned to the real world.

The alley was dimmer—and smellier—than its silent, scentless mirror. I exited quickly to the sidewalk.

The next high-rise on my path was Elozent. The "E" sculpture sat on its black base, no longer lit by the spotlights that used to make it gleam.

I paused in the dark plaza to check that the Eye was secure in my pocket.

This situation—the whole of it—would never have started if it weren't for the collapse of Elozent and the loss of my pension.

Bastards.

On the other hand . . . if it weren't for the collapse of Elozent and the loss of my pension, I'd have never gone through with dragging out those old books. Never searched for the ingredients to cast the spells. Never found my new friend, the key—it pulsed once, as if acknowledging the credit—never ventured to the witches' bar, never stole the Eye of the Elements from the museum.

How could I possibly show my appreciation?

I pictured the "E" sculpture engulfed in billowing, super-heated flames.

I had almost turned to walk away when the Eye did *something*. Power pulsed through me, invisibly, as if it had launched itself from my own body and into the night air.

There was nothing—only silence and stillness—for a count of two seconds.

Then the "E" sculpture exploded.

I staggered back and covered my face on instinct.

I should have run. Instead, I slowly lowered my arms.

The clear material had half-melted into a smoking slag that coated the base like burning lava. Multicolored flames crawled over the remnants. An acrid odor drifted across the plaza.

Something was bubbling up inside me. At first I thought it was my stomach, driven to spasm with the stress of the night.

No, it wasn't that.

It was a laugh.

The laugh shook my chest before the sound came out. When the sound finally did come out, I hardly recognized it as my own. I roared like I'd just heard the funniest joke ever invented. I was alive, and free, and younger in spirit than I could ever remember being.

I had to reel it in, though, when the light of the burning Elozent symbol attracted a small crowd from the late-night passersby.

I edged out of the light, dodged the lookie-loos, and headed for home.

Safely back in my condo, I pulled out the Eye and set it on the table. I'd have to be very, very careful not to touch it and think fiery thoughts. I didn't want to burn the condo building down.

I gingerly picked it up and took it down the hall to the bathroom. I set it on the counter and opened the shower curtain. Then I touched the Eye with one finger and pictured a stream of water hitting the shower wall.

The resulting stream hit the wall with the force of a garden hose and rebounded to soak my entire front with water.

I giggled like I'd been tickled.

I picked up the Eye—less gingerly this time—and boogied down the hallway to my lone potted plant. I scooped up the pot and cradled it in my arms, singing "Earth Angel" as I rocked it back and forth. I set it down in the kitchen next to a two-quart stainless steel saute pan.

I held the Eye before me and focused on the potting soil, imagining it lifting upward out of the pot. There was a bit of resistance—like pulling on a full garbage bag stuck in the can—before the soil tugged free, bringing the plant with it.

The soil and the plant floated in midair, gently shedding bits of dirt over the pot.

I veered my hand from the floating plant to the empty air over the saute pan, as if pulling the plant from one location to another. Again, I met resistance, but softer this time, and only for a moment before the plant drifted serenely over the shiny saute pan.

I let go, and the plant dropped into the pan with a thump and a small spray of dirt on the kitchen counter.

I set the Eye on the counter and clapped with delight. Fire, water, earth—I had more and better magic than *she* ever had.

Now, if only it worked for one more thing . . .

I eyed the ceiling speculatively. If I tried to fly, would I blast right into it? My upstairs neighbor wouldn't appreciate a new hole in the floor—and my skull certainly wouldn't appreciate being used as a battering ram.

I scooped up the Eye in one hand and cradled it to my chest securely.

I pictured my feet lifting smoothly from the floor, like Mary Poppins with her umbrella.

I ended up pitching sideways like the Tin Man. I grabbed the counter just in time to avoid crashing to the floor.

It was less like flying than like wearing a pair of roller skates with lubricated wheels.

I got my feet back under myself and concentrated on a little more lift for the rest of me.

That did the trick. I floated upward, bobbing in midair like it was water.

I laughed in relief—and got dropped unceremoniously to the floor. "Ow." I massaged my knees, then straightened up. Bedtime beckoned, but bedtime could wait.

One more try.

I lifted off again, carefully, and found my center of balance. "Oh, ho, ho! There we go." I floated around the couch and reached for the hallway. My aim was slightly off, though, and I managed to knock my shoulder a good one—but I stayed up, bobbing slightly and pushing off against the hallway walls.

I made it all the way to the bedroom without smacking into anything else. I tipped forward, floated over the bed, and let myself fall.

Boing! The mattress bounced with the impact, and I laughed for joy.

I rolled over to the nightstand and picked up my phone. An internet search revealed the phone number for Millefleur Properties, far to the north in Sparkle Beach. No one would be picking up the phone at this hour.

Perfect. I pressed the dial button.

The recording played: "Thank you for calling Millefleur Properties. Our office is closed at this time. Please leave your message after the tone."

Not *her* voice. But she'd hear the message, all the same.

"This message is for my sister." I took a breath. "Hilda—remember when you told me 'that's not how it works'? Well, guess what—I *made* it work. So, you can sit and spin!" I hung up.

Petty but fun.

This was going to be a cakewalk.

15

My accidental fire stunt brought Elozent back to the front page of the next day's newspaper, but it was the museum theft that took the headline: *Costumed Thief Steals Valuable Artifact at Museum Gala.*

If only they knew—the precious Eye of the Elements was tucked away in the shadow world, right next to the scarf I'd carried in before to test out whether items would remain where they'd been put. I didn't need to carry the Eye around with me, after all. Not like the key, which stayed on its leather necklace, safely around my neck, even while I slept.

I sipped my cafecito, took a bite of a guava pastry, and turned the newspaper page. The paper rustled over the rickety wooden cafe table. I still liked a hard copy, even though the online edition was technically more convenient.

My pleasant cafe breakfast was interrupted by a buzzing sound.

I retrieved my phone.

A message from Mauricio: *Did they find you last night?*

I blinked before typing a response. *Did who find me?*

The police, he wrote. *They were interviewing everyone.*

I froze, not knowing what to respond.

I gave them your contact info, he continued.

I swigged the last of the coffee, then typed out *Thank you* like each keystroke was forging a chain.

You're welcome! he replied.

An image followed the text, displaying a business card with the Miami Police Department logo and the contact information of Detective Auguste Landry.

"Oh, goody." I slapped the newspaper shut and took an angry bite of the pastry, spilling sugar crystals down my front.

Seriously, though—what did I have to be worried about?

My fingerprints? Nonexistent.

My costume? Changed and discarded.

My sudden departure after the theft? Well, that was a little trickier, but easily explained by my—ha!—advanced age, and the need for an early bedtime.

Still . . . might as well prove myself to be a good citizen.

I punched the number from the business card into the phone keypad.

"Detective Landry, Miami P.D." He had a plush, cultured kind of Southern accent, as if he weren't from around Miami. Louisiana, maybe.

"Hi there, Detective Landry. This is Lenore Frost. My friend Mauricio said you wanted to talk to me about the gala last night?"

"Yes, ma'am, I did. And thank you for calling me back. That saved me from having to chase you down," he added, with a chuckle.

I let out a small laugh. "Well, of course. It's only my duty."

"I could not be more pleased to hear it. Mrs. Frost, would you mind coming down and talking with me for a few minutes? I know you're probably very busy, but—"

"It would be my pleasure, Detective." Was I pouring it on too thick? No, a man in his line of work probably appreciated a little extra politeness.

I could hear him scribbling something down. "Thank you kindly, ma'am. Can you swing by now, or should I put you down for later?"

"Now would be fine."

We hung up after the expected pleasantries.

I brushed the sugar off my blouse and checked my slacks for any stains or marks. My compact revealed that my hair still looked neatly braided, although my lipstick could use a touchup. I slipped a lipstick out of my purse and made the fix discreetly.

I double-checked to make sure I wasn't carrying anything incriminating—no gold, no Eye, no Wickham cash—then walked to the nearest Metro station to catch a train.

I took a window seat. The doors closed, the train slid forward, and trees whizzed past: sabal palms, queen palms, and a dozen more plants Sheridan had pointed out and I had promptly forgotten the names of. Buildings popped up and down, everything from flashy condo and office towers to lowly strip malls and plain warehouses in a row.

From the Government Center station, the police department was only a couple of blocks north.

Good thing I'd worn my trusty New Balance sneakers.

The police department stood solid and fortress-like, nowhere near as graceful and pretty as the public library. The receptionist alerted the detective to my arrival. I used my nervous energy to pace the plain lobby rather than sit.

"Mrs. Frost?"

I turned. I'd been expecting someone younger. Instead, I saw a man about my age, not tall, but well-formed, with muscular forearms on display beneath rolled-up dress shirt sleeves. Nicely shaped eyeglasses gave him a thoughtful look. Silver sprinkled like salt through his brown hair.

"It's 'Ms.' And please, call me Lenore."

He smiled. Though his demeanor was businesslike, his eyes had a bit of a twinkle. "Lenore, then. Shall we go to my office?" He gestured with an economy that had its own controlled grace.

I had to sway forward to get my feet moving. I hadn't been prepared for the detective to be . . . handsome?

He held the door for me, like a real Southern gentleman, and waited for me to sit before taking his own seat behind a desk piled with stacks of paper. "It isn't usually like this," he said, combining several stacks to clear space. "Incidents like these—they generate a lot of paperwork."

"I can imagine."

"So." He slapped a file onto the desk. "Let's start with the basics. Spell your name for me?"

I spelled it.

"Address?"

I gave him the condo address.

"Family?"

My thoughts jumped to my sister, who was hundreds of miles north. "Just my son."

He nodded and made a note, then looked up and made eye contact. "Your friend Mauricio said he saw you right before the theft last night."

"I don't know if I would have put it that way—"

"Forgive me. I mean he saw you at the gala last night, shortly before the theft was reported."

"Yes."

"And then after you saw him . . ."

"I left."

"You left." He made another note.

Our eyes met.

My heart started to beat faster. "I was tired." I forced a charming smile. "You know how it is at our age."

"Our age." The corner of his mouth lifted. "I like that." He held my gaze. "And where did you go after you left?"

"Home."

"Did you see anything on your way out?"

"No."

"Did you stop anywhere?"

I pictured the flaming Elozent sculpture. "No."

"Do you have any connection to Elozent Industries?"

That just about stopped my breath cold. "I used to work there."

"Oh?"

"Lost my job when everybody else did."

"I see." Lines appeared between his eyebrows, though the rest of his expression didn't change. "And how did you feel about that?"

"Is that relevant?"

"Humor me."

"It wasn't the greatest moment of my life, if that's what you're asking."

He nodded slowly, as if contemplating what I had said.

Silence descended. I waited for him to say something. When he didn't, I shifted to put my purse over my shoulder. "Is that all? Can I go?"

He blinked, then appeared to come back to himself. "Yes, I reckon that'll do for now. May I see you out?"

I stood. "I know the way."

He got to his feet and opened the door for me.

I walked out.

"Oh—Ms. Frost?"

I looked back. "Lenore."

He snapped his fingers as if in jest at his own poor memory. "Lenore, yes."

He wasn't fooling anyone.

"What were you wearing that night?" he continued.

My eyebrows rose. "A witch costume, like everyone else."

"Right." The way he lingered on the word made it hard to tell if he doubted me, or if he was just prone to dragging out vowels. The hint of amusement in his eyes didn't help. "You have a good day, Ms.—Lenore."

I held his gaze. "Likewise, Detective."

16

A cold front passed through the next day. The thick clouds darkened the sky even earlier than normal for the time of year. Rain pattered on the condo windows while I put on light layers topped with my water-resistant jacket. I threaded a strand of leather through the Eye, then fastened it to my braid crown like a hair ornament. Tied securely, it would be in reach, difficult to touch accidentally, and impossible to drop.

I pulled up my hood, then pressed my hand over the key hiding beneath my shirt.

I was ready.

I picked up my phone, but hesitated. Would my son notice anything amiss? What would I tell him?

The same reassuring things as always. He had no reason to believe anything else.

"Hey, there," I said when Sheridan picked up. "Thought

I'd check in a little early so you didn't have to worry about calling me."

Pots and pans rattled in the background. "Oh, okay—I was going to call you after dinner."

"Don't let me interrupt you—"

"No, it's fine. You're okay? You took your medicine?"

"Of course I did. I'm very responsible, you know." Other than the whole breaking-and-entering thing. "In fact, I'm going to spend a quiet evening at home, reading."

He chuckled. "Don't do anything I wouldn't do."

"Would you read a Jackie Collins novel?"

"I might."

"Well, then. We're in good shape. Don't let me keep you—go eat your dinner."

"Yes, Mother."

I groaned. "You make me sound a hundred years old when you say it like that."

"Sure, Mom."

"Now you sound like a teenager. I guess that puts me back in my mid-forties." I smiled. "I'll take it. Love you."

"Love you, too. Don't forget about the Trail or Treat tomorrow."

"I won't."

We said our goodbyes and hung up. I left the phone on the table.

I locked up and took the elevator down. Rain lashed the ground outside the lobby door. I tugged my hood tighter and headed out on the empty sidewalk. No one wanted to be out on a literally dark and stormy night.

I hurried to the Elozent tower, taking care not to slip on the wet sidewalks. The air smelled of salt and wet concrete. Rivers of water raced through the gutters beside me.

By the time I reached the tower, rain had gathered on the edge of my hood. It dripped into my face as I gazed at the observation deck. It was *so* high. I'd practiced flying around the condo with no problem at all, but this was another level altogether.

If I somehow slipped into the shadow world while flying high . . . and the magic of the Eye didn't work there—

I didn't even want to think about it.

I pulled the key out from under my shirt and placed it between the layers of my shirt and the jacket. That way, it wouldn't touch my skin and get activated by accident.

One last check: no one in sight.

I placed my hand on the Eye of the Elements—securely tied to my hair—and concentrated on lifting myself, just as I'd practiced.

My feet left the ground. I tipped slightly forward and found my center of gravity, then pushed upward. I rose one floor high, but the wind sent me drifting backwards, away from the building. For a moment, I was lost in the mist and rain—my stomach flip-flopped before I caught sight of the glossy Elozent windows and managed to get closer without smashing myself into them like a bug on a windshield.

I floated upward.

Two stories, then three and four. Then I lost track; the floors extended above and below me out of sight as if they went on forever in both directions.

If I couldn't see the ground, then no one on the ground could see me.

A shift in the swirling wind cleared the view to the observation deck for the blink of an eye.

I was almost there.

I tightened my grip on the Eye and pushed the magic harder, faster. It surged around me and lifted me like a giant's hand. For the first time, I forgot my terror—I was *flying*. I would reach the deck, I would waltz into the executive offices, and I would take whatever I wanted, whatever I *needed*, to prove what the executives had done and regain my lost retirement.

All I had to do was make it *that much* further.

Then—the lifting sensation shuddered.

I bounced in midair. One hand went to the rain-slicked windows as if I could grab on to the glass. Instead, my palm squeaked downward as I lost altitude an inch at a time.

Panic shot through me.

So *close*. Just a little more—

I held on to the Eye and poured my every thought into rising. I rose with a sickly surge that knocked me sideways into the glass. Half-stunned, I reeled away and lost sight of the building.

In the moments hanging in mid-air, I saw my son waiting for me at Black Mangrove Preserve. Waiting for a mother who would never arrive. How long would he be at the Trail or Treat, checking the time and growing ever more worried?

The observation deck lay only a few floors above.

Maybe I could make it.

Or maybe the magic would fail, and I would fall.

I closed my eyes. "I have to try," I said, to a Sheridan who wasn't there to hear me.

You don't have the magic. You'll never have the magic.

"Yes, I do!"

Lightning blasted the side of the building with a flash of light, followed by thunder that shook my whole body.

I lurched upward in fits and starts. The railing of the observation deck appeared above me. I reached for the slick metal and slipped. My heart flew into my throat—the last thing I would see, I was sure, was the burned remains of the "E" sculpture before it destroyed my body just like it had my retirement.

How my sister would shake her head at me. Poor Lenore, playing with things she didn't understand.

In one final surge, the Eye blasted me up and over the railing. I landed ungracefully on all fours, scraped and knocked about but alive. I groped for the key. "Shadow world," I huffed.

Sweet, blessed relief. The driving rain vanished. The darkness lifted. I'd never been so glad to see that cold, gray light. I could have kissed the gray pavers beneath my feet. Instead, I rolled onto my back and gazed up at the tranquil white haze of the sky.

I did it.

I, Lenore Frost, flew to the top of a skyscraper.

And now, I would ransack it.

I stretched, rolled halfway over, and pushed myself into a sitting position. I stood and crossed the observation deck.

The double doors to the executive floor swung open in silence.

Where to begin?

The coffee bar stood abandoned in the center of the space. The inner hallways most likely held little of interest; managers at Mauricio's level, as lofty as they may have been in comparison to the rest of us, were still just cogs in the machine. No, if anything was to be found, it would be found in the window offices, with their thick carpet, leather furniture, and sweeping views—where one Robert Wickham, CEO, spent his days before bailing out and leaving the rest of us to suffer.

I knew exactly where to find it even without the nameplate—brass, in real life, but it appeared to be silver in this black-and-white alternate reality.

The door opened easily.

I immediately went to the desk and pulled open the center drawer: a few blank Elozent notepads and a handful of cheap pens, as sparse as a hotel desk. I slammed the center drawer shut.

The deep right hand drawer yielded a row of empty file folders. I ripped them out of the frame and pitched them into the air in case there was something hidden beneath. The folders fell and littered the floor.

Nothing hidden.

The top left hand drawer held an old Swingline stapler.

The bottom left hand drawer held an Elozent stress ball.

I slammed my palms on the desktop. How was I supposed to find some sort of smoking gun when the desk was as clean as if it had never been used?

I seized the Elozent stress ball, growled, and pitched it against the window.

It bounced off harmlessly and rolled to a stop against the wall, where an abstract painting hung.

A painting?

I left the desk and seized the artwork by the frame. It swung away from the wall, like a cabinet door.

Behind it—

A safe!

I caressed the dial. Spun it a few times.

Would it be more treasure? Or, better still, a second set of accounting books? A collection of incriminating USB drives?

I pulled the lever, which made a satisfying *clunk*.

The door swung open.

A ledger lay within. I slid it free, carried it to the empty desk, and opened the plain cover.

No title page. No introduction. No heading.

Just a list.

Page after page after page of handwritten names and addresses.

I frowned. "I went through all this for some kind of Rolodex?" I flipped faster. Alabama, Alaska, Arizona. Alphabetical by state, then. Connecticut, Delaware . . . Florida. I ran my finger down the page of unfamiliar names and addresses.

Then I gasped.

Hildegarde Millefleur, 1153 Atlantic Avenue, Sparkle Beach, FL.

My sister?

17

What the hell was my sister's name and address doing in a handwritten ledger in the safe of the Elozent CEO?

And who were all these other people?

I fanned through the pages, looking for clues, but found nothing.

I sank into the leather chair and spun to face the window. Biscayne Bay glowed silver beneath the bleached gray-white sky. Then I put my feet up on the CEO's desk—why not?—and leaned back.

Hilda.

The real witch of the family.

Hadn't spoken to her in decades—except for that one voicemail message. Estranged didn't even begin to cover it. Hadn't even told her about Sheridan.

Not that she'd care, or couldn't find out on her own, if she really wanted to.

She was up north, living the high life. Gifted with magic—fire magic and the mind-manipulation that came with it—and married into wealth. By all accounts she did quite well for herself, was even considered something of a local dignitary, if the papers were to be believed.

And now here she was, connected to Robert Wickham, the one person I could have possibly hated even more than her.

I picked up a pen and tapped it against my lips. The real question was: was Hilda on Wickham's good list? A co-conspirator in some strange way?

Or was this directory something else?

I ran the pen down the Florida page again, looking for more Sparkle Beach addresses. Nothing else rang a bell.

How about the Miami addresses?

A quick scan revealed no familiar names, although the first name "Tuesday" jumped out at me, purely for being unusual.

It wasn't what I'd come for—it wasn't a smoking gun—but this list had been valuable to Robert Wickham, and therefore it was valuable to me.

I had to have it—but how?

If I popped into reality and took it, I might show up on a hidden surveillance camera. There had been enough of that back at the museum, and I didn't need any additions to my trail of evidence. Especially if I'd been filmed when I landed on the observation deck.

Still—I couldn't imagine leaving the ledger behind. Not with my sister's name in it and me not knowing why. It wouldn't surprise me if she was as much a villain as he was, but—

On the off chance that there was something else going on . . .

I closed the ledger and returned to the safe.

This was a logic puzzle. If I tried to take the shadow of the real ledger into the real world, it would disappear like that gray chocolate pumpkin I tried to steal from Parallel 26.

If I flipped to the real world, the real ledger would be locked in a safe I couldn't possibly open.

The only way to save the information would be to copy it to something real and *then* return to the real world.

I patted my many pockets. In an attempt to travel light, I'd emptied almost all of them—except for one, which held my normal keys, a packet of Elozent-branded sticky notes, and a single blue Elozent pen. I sighed with relief.

I reopened the ledger and compared the number of pages to the number of sticky notes. I had nowhere near enough sticky notes to copy everything. But I did have enough for every single name and address in the Florida section.

I set to work and copied until my hand cramped. I shook it out and continued. When I finished, I had a very riffled stack of sticky notes, filled front and back with slightly smudged writing. I carefully tucked the notes in my pocket along with the pen.

A search of the other window offices yielded top-shelf liquor hidden in bottom drawers and a few Cuban cigars. Nothing even close to incriminating. They'd obviously cleaned everything out ahead of time.

I returned to the observation deck.

The ground looked terribly far away.

I'd barely made it up. There was no way the Eye would carry me back down. It seemed to have run out of power.

If I wanted to stay in the shadows—to remain unseen—the only way down was the stairs. I drummed my fingers on the shiny railing. "Couldn't anything go according to plan? Maybe just once?"

There was no other way.

I headed for the stairs and pushed open the door. The stairs spiraled up and down from the landing like a dizzying shot from a Hitchcock movie.

The sound of my footsteps echoed strangely. The first few floors down weren't so bad, nowhere near as hard as climbing up. Halfway down, I sat on a stair to stop my head from spinning from the constant turns. When my stomach stopped roiling, I got up and kept going.

By the time I reached the ground floor, I'd never been so glad I'd stayed in decent shape by walking to and from work.

I pushed the ground floor exit door open and stepped into the empty hall leading to the lobby. The metal detector stood unattended, the same dull gray it had been in reality. I passed through it and exited the building.

My legs wobbled a bit as the adrenalin wore off, and my left knee started letting me know it wasn't too happy with having to climb down thirty-one flights of stairs.

"Shut up, knee." I tried not to limp while crossing the Elozent plaza.

The walk home took longer than usual.

I went straight to my car. The door opened and I let myself fold across the front seats. I was tempted to take a nap right there in the shadow world, right in the front seat of my car—but with home only steps away, I rallied the energy to make the switch.

I tucked the key into my shirt once more, pressed it into contact with my skin, and imagined the real, colorful world.

Raindrops pattered on the car windows.

I was back.

I sat up cautiously, wary of observers. The rain had provided plenty of cover, though. I grabbed an umbrella from the back seat and hurried to the condo lobby door. I shook off the umbrella, pushed the elevator button, and nodded to the Patrick Nagel lady.

I think she approved of breaking into skyscrapers.

Safely inside my condo, I pulled out the sticky notes and laid them on the table.

My phone was flashing.

I picked it up and carried it to the sofa, where I took off my sneakers and socks before checking the notification.

I heard about Elozent, Sheridan had written. *Are you okay?*

I blinked at the screen. About Elozent? Would that be the company collapse, the theft from the Elozent-sponsored gala, the burning "E," or—God forbid—the mysterious person spotted on the observation deck?

I shook my head. No, that last one couldn't have possibly got out yet. *I'm fine*, I typed, hoping to end the conversation there.

You didn't tell me, he replied. *I saw it on the news.*

Though it was impossible to read the tone from a text message, he sounded kind of hurt. I sighed, then typed: *I didn't want to worry you.*

Do you need money?

I pictured the secret outdoor stash. *No.*

Several seconds passed before his response. *We'll talk about it more tomorrow.*

"Not if I can help it," I said. I discarded the phone and exchanged my rain-soaked clothes for dry ones. I should have changed into pajamas, but I had enough adrenaline to power a city—and several questions for Sondra.

Time for a return trip to Magic City Tiki.

I'd have to risk carrying the Eye with me.

The rain scattered light across my windshield as I drove back to the artsy neighborhood. Although the downpour should have driven everyone away, the place was absolutely packed. Music thumped louder than the first time I visited.

I pushed through the crowd to reach the bar.

No sign of Sondra.

I waved at the bartender to get her attention. "Excuse me—have you seen Sondra?"

The bartender set down a glass and leaned closer to be heard over the din. "Who?"

"Sondra," I nearly shouted. "The witch in the cloud?" I mimed vaping.

"Oh, *Sondra.* Over there." The bartender waved toward a far corner and returned to mixing a drink.

I found Sondra alone at a table for two. Vapor swirled around her throne-like wicker chair, preserving the space for herself despite the crowd and the overall lack of seating.

I slid onto a smaller seat opposite her.

Her cool gaze met mine. "Well done."

I leaned in. "What do you mean, 'Well done'?"

She smiled, lazy and catlike, and blew a cloud in my face.

I coughed and waved it away.

"Can't I congratulate you?"

"You could try lowering your voice."

She waved a dismissive hand. "They have no idea."

"They will if you're too carefree about it."

"I'm never carefree." Sondra blew a controlled cloud. "So tell me—how did it go?"

"It was . . ." I stopped to collect my thoughts. Her eyes were altogether too bright. "It was fine. But I have some questions."

"Such as?"

"What do you do when it runs out of power?"

Sondra laid one hand on the table, turned it palm-up, and wiggled her long fingers. She looked at me expectantly.

I sighed. "How much?"

"How much is it worth to you?"

My lips pursed. This damn witch. I rummaged in my purse for all the remaining cash I had on me and passed it over.

She swiftly tucked it away under her neckline. "You'll have to recharge it."

"I could have figured that out without forking over a wad of cash. How exactly am I supposed to do that?"

She shrugged. "Convince someone to give you some of their magic, I suppose."

"How about you?"

Sondra laughed. "No, thanks."

"It's impossible, then."

"Oh, I don't know. Leverage is *everything*." Sondra sipped her drink and eyed me over the rim.

"How do you know all this, anyway?"

"Let's just say I learned it in the school of hard knocks." She said it lightly, but her knuckles whitened as she gripped her glass.

Curiouser and curiouser. "Is that where you learned to have no qualms whatsoever about the Wickhams losing their precious artifact?"

"I could say the same of you." She blew a sharp stream of vapor. "But, yes—it is. And if you ever see Robert Wickham—"

"I don't think I ever would—"

"You can tell him Sondra said so." A mad giggle escaped her lips.

"Um . . . yeah." Sondra seemed to be a few ingredients short of a full potion. "Do you think I could get in touch with you somehow, if I was out of town?"

Sondra blinked, then pulled a tiny flip phone from her sleeve. She waved it at me. "My burner. Do you have a burner?" She flipped it open and peered at the screen. "Very handy for when you want to disappear." She gripped her vape pen in her teeth, pulled a real pen from somewhere, and seized my forearm.

"Whoa, there—"

She wrote a phone number in ink on my skin, then dropped the ink pen and took her vape pen back in hand.

"Uh, thanks."

Sondra puffed out a cloud and said nothing.

I slowly slid out of the booth. I paid the wild lights and music no mind as I walked out. I knew where I could get the magic I needed.

It was time to finish this.

It was time to go *home.*

18

I had one last obligation to fulfill the following day, and it required a replacement witch hat since I'd abandoned the two from the gala. Even before the Trail or Treat start time, cars filled the Black Mangrove Preserve parking lot. I made my way past little mermaids, pint-sized superheroes, and a bunch more kids wearing costumes I didn't even recognize.

Sheridan stood at the first treat station. He secured a Robin Hood hat over his tousled hair and waved.

I gave his arm a light punch. "Steal from the rich and give to the poor, huh?"

"No theft. This candy was donated. Here—have a bag." He ripped open an oversized bag and handed it to me.

"Mmm," I said, poking around the variety pack. "Don't mind if I do." I seized a miniature 3 Musketeers bar and tore it open.

"I didn't mean you should scarf it, Mom."

"I don't work for free, kiddo. You're paying me in chocolate." I ate the candy in two bites. Something about climbing down thirty-one flights had given me an appetite. I held the bag out to him and gave it a little shake. "Come to the dark side. We have Mars Bars."

He laughed and took one. "Fine. You've corrupted me. Now sharpen up—we have customers."

The parade of trick-or-treaters didn't let up for quite some time. In a brief moment between rushes, I turned to the backstocked candy bags, snagged another 3 Musketeers, and stuffed it in my mouth.

"Hey, lady—is that your real witch costume?"

I whipped around to find Thanos Boy staring at me with undisguised curiosity. At least, it would have probably looked like undisguised curiosity if he hadn't been wearing a large purple plastic head.

Sheridan's gaze traveled from the boy to me. "You two know each other?"

I tried in vain to swallow the bite.

It stuck in my throat.

"Sure we do," said Thanos Boy. "I helped her climb out of—"

"A bad mood," I said, finally forcing down the sticky chocolate. "He helped me climb out of a bad mood one day, isn't that right?"

Thanos Boy opened his mouth to speak.

I grabbed the nearest bag of candy and poured the entire thing into his pumpkin bucket. "Happy Halloween!" I waved him along. "Next!"

Sheridan stared at me.

"What?"

"You just dumped an entire industrial-sized bag of candy into that kid's bucket."

"So?"

"So . . ."

"Oh, lighten up. I made his night." I refused to make eye contact; instead, I carefully dropped exactly two pieces of candy in the next kid's bucket. "See? I'll behave."

"Uh-huh." He looked at me for one beat longer. Then he returned to doling out candy.

"Listen," I said. "I think I might get out of town for a while. Take a little vacation."

Whatever weird look he'd been giving me before suddenly multiplied by ten. "Since when do you even leave the greater Miami area? What brings this on?"

"I'm retired now, Sheridan." I summoned a chipper tone. "I can see the world!"

"And what about Elozent?"

"What about it?"

"The news said—"

"You can't believe everything you see on the TV. I'm *fine*."

Skepticism twisted his lips. "You're fine?"

I dropped candy in the next bucket in time with my words: "I'm. Fine."

He shook his head. "If you say so."

We finished the Trail or Treat on lighter topics. After we cleaned up, Sheridan walked me to my car.

"When are you leaving?"

"I think I might get a head start tonight."

"Tonight?" He laughed in disbelief. "Who are you? And what have you done with my mother? At least tell me where you're going."

I didn't really want him to know, but I didn't see a way around it. "Sparkle Beach."

His eyebrows shot up. "Sparkle Beach? You told me you hated Sparkle Beach—*and* your sister. You two haven't even spoken in—"

"Yeah, well. It's time I came to terms with my past."

"I can't tell if that's a good thing or a bad thing."

"Neither can I."

He gave me a dubious look. "I'm still going to call you everyday."

"Oh, I'm sure you will."

"And you have to promise me you'll drive safely . . ."

"Kiddo, I'm not going to the moon." I removed his Robin Hood hat and tried in vain to smooth his hair. "Just back to where I came from."

We hugged before we parted.

The drive back to downtown Miami felt longer than usual. The early sunset threw a shadow over the landscape—swamp, suburb, and city alike. Back at my condo building, I nodded a greeting to the lady on the Patrick Nagel poster on my way upstairs. Upstairs, with witch hat and purse in hand, I headed down the hall toward my door.

Detective Auguste Landry stood right outside with his hand raised to knock.

I jumped backward a step.

He looked up at the sudden movement, then lowered his hand. "My apologies, Ms. Lenore. I didn't mean to startle you."

Oh, he had startled me, all right. Where had I left the Eye?

Sweat prickled across my skin.

Right—in the shadow world. It had joined the scarf. I left it there after coming home late from Magic City Tiki. I stopped myself from sighing in relief. "Can I help you?"

He glanced at my witch hat. "Is that your . . . Halloween costume?"

"What, this old thing?" I laughed and waved the hat like a coquettish girl with a fan. "This was just to help my son out at a Halloween event. Sheridan." I was babbling. I half-expected him to pull out a notebook and start writing it down. Then again, he seemed too smart to even need to write things down. "He's a forest ranger." I couldn't keep a note of pride out of my voice.

Another awkward silence.

I fumbled with my keys. "Is there something I can help you with?"

"Ms. Lenore, you didn't have any plans to leave town anytime soon, did you?" Either his eyes were twinkling, or his glasses were catching flickers of the hall lights.

The blood in my veins felt like ice water. "Why?"

"I may have a few more questions to ask you about the night at the gala."

"Why not ask them now?"

He gave an affable shrug. "I'm still working them out."

Bull. He hadn't stopped by on a Friday evening just to oh-by-the-way mention that he'd want to talk again soon.

He was trying to catch me off guard.

What was he reading on my face, with those clever eyes of his? What did he know? How could he possibly know *anything*? Suddenly, Sondra's burner phone seemed like an excellent idea. "Of course I'd be happy to answer your questions. Only I have plans to visit my sister, you see—" I don't know why it popped out. It just did.

"Your sister?" He was filing the information away, like a squirrel with an acorn.

"Yes, my sister." I silently cursed the impatience that had crept into my voice.

He paused, keeping his gaze on mine. "Family is important."

"So is hitting the road on time."

"Of course." Again, that courtly Southern tone. "I wouldn't dream of stopping you, Ms. Lenore. You do have my card?"

I arched an eyebrow. "Sure I do, Detective. I'll call you when I need company." Oh, boy. What was wrong with me? The man was *investigating* me, and I was *flirting* with him.

He chuckled. "I look forward to it."

Great. If he didn't think I was a criminal, maybe he'd ask me out. I cleared my throat. "I should be going."

"Au revoir, then, as they say."

"Happy Halloween, Detective." I slid the key into the lock, opened the door, slipped inside, and shut it. The lock clicked home. I leaned against the door and quietly exhaled.

Leaving Miami sounded better and better.

Good thing my bag was already packed.

I walked to the window. I wouldn't be seeing this view for a while: buildings rising over a grid of palm-lined streets; the waters of the bay shimmering under an autumn moon.

My city.

Cosmopolitan.

Tropical.

A world away from Sparkle Beach, the small town I swore I'd never go back to. The route north unfurled like a black ribbon in my mind.

My sister had the magic I needed, and I intended to get it.

No matter what it took.

KATE MOSEMAN
Silver
Spells